# Her Way or No Way

by Carson Mackenzie

Published by CM Books, LLC
Copyright © April 2018 Carson Mackenzie
Reissued/Reedited/Extended Version August 2021
Cover Design by Carson Mackenzie, CM Cover Designs
ISBN# 978-1-952184-39-0 Paperback

author.

If you find any books being sold or shared illegally, please contact the author at carsonmackenzieauthor2020@gmail.com.

# Synopsis

O'Hagan's gym has been a part of the south side community of Chicago for decades. Kearney O'Hagan's family has owned the gym since his great-grandfather emigrated to the city from Ireland. Most men in his shoes with only a daughter to carry on the tradition of turning out some of the best fighters would worry about the end to a legacy—but most men didn't have a daughter like Teagan.

Teagan O'Hagan grew up in her father's gym. She was used to taking a ribbing from the men who train there, and it never has bothered her. At least not until the two friends joined and questioned Teagan's role at the place, leaving her wondering if it is their questions or the fact, she is attracted to them that has her temper flaring.

Maximum Masetti and Nicolo Asaro are best friends and cousins who train together, each for a different weight class. The small-time fights bring them extra cash, but they have their sights on the big league.  However, to get there, they need a trainer/manager and a gym to back them. When they think they have found the perfect place, their attraction to the fiery redhead who works in the gym could be their personal downfall, one they are willing to take.

While the attraction grows into more than either party expects—Teagan shows Max and Nico that if they're going to succeed in the MMA to the next level, it will be Her Way or No Way.

# Contents

# Prologue

## Teagan

The crowd was minimal at the civic center for the amateur tournament. I'd been there most of the day watching the fights.

"Hey, babe. Is O'Hagan's looking for some fighters to recruit?"

"Stop calling me babe. And I could ask you the same question." Christoph Kiev sat down in the seat beside me.

"Such a hard ass, Teagan. But yeah, I'm here to scope out some fresh talent, same as you. I take on a couple new fighters every year. Have to keep things fresh." He leaned back in his seat.

"Yeah, must be tough to handle your business and meet the demands of the circuit." It hadn't been a question, but the sarcasm would be lost on Christoph. I had never met anyone whose ego surpassed his, and I spent my days surrounded my men.

"It is. If I had a decent trainer who could work my guys while I was competing, it would make shit a lot easier. When is your old man going to sell to me? If it's the boxing side, hell, I told you I'd set an area aside just for him to do that at my gym. I'm more interested in getting you as a trainer for the MMA guys. You're outgrowing your dad's gym, Teagan."

"Ah, was that a compliment? I'm touched. I could probably get my dad to go for it..." That got the asshole's attention. "...sometime between now and say fucking never."

"You wound me, Teagan." Christoph placed his hand over his heart to emphasize his hurt.

"Yeah, right. Why are you really here? Other than to aggravate me." His smirk told me he had an interest in the last two fights of the day because I hadn't seen him milling around earlier. I knew he had to be interested in at least a couple of the last four fighters. Christoph's arrogance wouldn't allow him to keep his motives to himself. Being the schmuck he was.

The fighters for the light heavyweight took to the ring. And I looked them over. As my eyes hit on the dark haired one, my stomach tightened. He was tall, maybe six one or two with a broad chest that narrowed as it led down to his waist, the 'V' prominent even with the shorts on. One thigh was bigger than my own waist, and that was saying something considering I wasn't a delicate flower.

I followed his movement as he bounced on the toes of his feet, his skin already showed signs of exertion with the slight sheen to it. When he reached down and adjusted the front of his shorts, I blinked. He seemed to be big all over.

"The jock must be pinching his family jewels," Christoph's voice had me turning in his direction.

"Seriously, that is what you focus on?" He had to have been watching me as I scoped out the fighter.

"Asaro, he has the strength but lacks in the basic techniques every fighter needs. He will win but only at this level. Unless you are interested in his other attributes." Christoph smirked, and I wanted to smack the look right off his face.

"Grow up, Christoph. Don't you have somewhere else to be, like I don't know, another planet? Or Hell?"

"Only if you will come away with me. Come on, Teagan. Your knowledge, my ability, we would be unstoppable in this industry. And on a personal level...I think we could be explosive. When are you at least going to take me up on the offer of dinner?"

*Yep, the bile was working its way up.*

"How the hell do you fight, even walk, with the size of your head?" I turned back to the fight in time to watch Asaro take the other fighter to the mat. The move could have been smoother, but the result was the same.

"Because the size of my other head helps

balance me." Well, the tingling I got from watching Asaro take down his opponent left in a flash. It was replaced with acidy bile. I had to uncap my water bottle and take a drink to wash the nasty taste down.

"Go away, Christoph. I'm sure you can find another woman, or ten, who would jump at the chance to jump you. I'm just not one of them."

He leaned toward me. "Teagan, we'll see how fast that changes when O'Hagan's doesn't get sanctioned, and you are looking for a place to go. You think if you fill your gym with fighters from the different weight classes that you'll have a chance. That is only part of it, O'Hagan's is outdated. My offer will be there, Teagan, both of them." He winked and stood. "Heard Daly is ready to fight. He will get the only shot at my fighter, Crav, before his first sanctioned fight. You know, since your man will never get that far. You need true talent, not these types." He lifted his chin toward the ring, "They will only ever be amateurs." He turned and started to walk away.

"Whatever. Later, Christoph." He turned his head and gave me a chin lift. I turned back to the ring to watch the two fighters land on the mat. This time the other one was unable to buck Asaro off. Asaro straddled him, and with a beefy forearm position at the other's throat and a few punches to the guy's ribs, he gave up and hit the mat. The win to Asaro in two rounds. Lack of finesse maybe, but some skill—Christoph was full of shit. It was there.

Asaro just needed to fine-tune his mechanics a little, and then he would be a force.

The ring was cleared and then readied for the last fight, the heavyweight matchup. I noticed Asaro took a seat off to the side of the ring instead of going to the locker rooms. He held an ice pack to his cheek from a blow to the face he had taken. The two heavyweights entered the ring, and the one looked over at Asaro and gave a chin lift. Asaro gave him a thumb's up in return, and the fighter grinned. Their looks were similar enough the two could be brothers, but when the announcer gave the introductions, the heavyweight's last name was Masetti. Maximum Masetti.

Masetti was big. I estimated between two thirty or two fifty. He had to be pushing the weight max. He was tall, too. I'd guess at least six three or four. When the announcer read off the stats, I had hit close on his height and was barely off on the weight as he came in at two forty-eight. My stomach tightened just as it had when I looked Asaro over. Masetti's chest was wide, his shoulders broader. His arms were massive, and he had tree trunks as thighs. The 'V' leading into his shorts wasn't as pronounced as Asaro's but still impressive. I needed to get my mind off the two fighters' bodies and remember what I was there for. Fighters to train, that was all. The urge to run my fingers through his hair was as ridiculous as the thought of the taste of his skin.

The fight started and was over in under the

13

first three minutes. Masetti had only taken two solid hits and a kick from his opponent when he lunged straight for the other fighter. He wrapped the guy up and slammed him to the mat, his own body followed, and he landed on top. After he had pushed himself to a sitting position, he drawn back his arm and with a forward motion, he landed the blow on the fighter's chin before the fighter had a chance to block it. The fighter's head was turned to the side by the force of the blow. Masetti had knocked him out.

I sat in my seat and watched the referee give the win to Masetti. After everyone around me had started to make their way to the exit, I watched Masetti give Asaro a man hug. The two men grinned wide at each other, and I was stunned. The expression changed their looks from handsome to downright gorgeous. No man should be allowed to look that hot. I shook my head, stood, and started toward the exit. The day hadn't been a total bust, I'd found some raw talent.

At least in two fighters.

By the time I left and reached my vehicle, I wasn't sure how they would fit in at O'Hagan's Gym, which made me mad at myself, because I didn't know if I had come to a conclusion solely on their ability or their effect on me. Feeling that way was new territory for me.

What I did know as I started my truck—they would benefit the gym. However, my gut said the cost to me could outweigh the benefit.

# Chapter One

## Max

The noise from the crowd was ear-splitting to the point the floor vibrated in the United Center as Nico and I waited for the fighters to enter the ring. We'd watched the three previous fights for the lower weight classes but had two more left before the weight classes we competed in took to the ring.

"Damn, I've not seen one fighter so far that we couldn't hang with," Nico said and turned toward me.

"Yeah, but we've only seen the lower weight classes. The light heavyweight and heavyweight fights are the last of the night," I said just as the welterweight match was announced to start in twenty minutes.

"Max, we've seen all four of the fighters in those two matches before. You know, and I know, we are just as good. We just haven't had the

15

opportunity to fight them to prove it," Nico said and opened the program to read the bios and fight records of the two men who were up next.

"I heard of Matvi Crav, he's from Kiev's Gym, which shouldn't be a shocker considering they always have a fighter in one or more of the classes, it's typical. Especially since Christoph Kiev owns the gym. The Daly guy, I've never heard the name before. You?" I asked as Nico continued to flip through the flyer.

"Nah, but the gym that sponsors him, I have, so have you. Don't you remember my dad talking about it a couple months back at Sunday dinner?" I shook my head no, and Nico continued. "O'Hagan's Gym, the one on the south side, it's one of the oldest around. The owner/manager there was some up-and-coming boxer back in the day. Can't remember what Dad said happened. Anyway, he stopped competing and started running the gym full time. He's turned out quite a few boxing contenders over the years, too. They're trying to get sanctioned by the MMA, but rumor has it they're having a hard time, some of it has to do with them doing things old school. You know, basic equipment, not like the innovated equipment most gyms offer."

"Yeah, I do remember that. Didn't Uncle Vinnie say something about the old man having a new trainer?" I asked, and Nico rolled the program and shoved it in his back pocket.

"I don't recall. Man, I hope this fight and the

16

next one goes by fast, because we've got work in the morning, and I don't want to be here 'til midnight," Nico said with a yawn.

"Yeah, Mom and Aunt Angelina weren't happy when they found out we were working on Sunday." I shook my head and then chuckled because I knew my dad and Nico's dad were going to hear about that for the next few months. In our mothers' eyes, Sunday was for family.

Our families owned M&A Construction, the M for Masetti, which was my family, and the A for Asaro, which was Nico's family. My dad, Frank, and Nico's mom, Angelina, were brother and sister, making us family on top of being best friends. We even shared the same birthday, having been born only fifteen minutes apart.

"All that damn rain last week put us behind. We have to get the rest of the frame up so we can get that bitch under roof," I said just as they announced the names of the fighters for the next bout.

"We should be able to do that in the next couple of days. I just hope we get caught up and back on schedule. The bonus in the contract for coming in on time or early with the build would be nice," Nico said, and we turned our heads to watch as Matvi Crav and his crew made their way to the ring.

"It would be. It will also help once we officially start training. I hate to leave the family shorthanded, but there's no way we will be able to work full time and train like we need to. We're only going to be able to help on our down time. We've wanted this for a while, Nico, and now is as good as any to go for it. We need a gym to take us on, that's the only way we are going to make this a profession. If we don't, we will stay at the local tournament level. I would prefer a gym with a good trainer and a manager who knows what the hell is going on. We are in the best physical shape we have ever been in. Training together, the martial arts classes, and sparring with each other along with the wrestling has gotten us to this point. It's just not going to be enough to take us to the top," I said, and Nico agreed as we watched the other fighter and his group make their way to the ring from the opposite side.

Shawn Daly stepped into the ring and exposed the woman who had been walking behind him. At Nico's "Fuck me," I knew that he had seen her, too. She wore a green O'Hagan's t-shirt with black leggings, and her red hair looked to have blonde streaks when the lights shined on it. She had it pulled back in a ponytail that put her flawless complexion in full view. The woman was a knockout. I couldn't see her eyes from where I sat, but they could've been any color and it wouldn't have mattered.

I watched as she leaned in and said something, and Daly nodded his head and winked at her.

"We have been competing in the wrong tournaments because damn, just damn," I said as

18

she stepped back and stood beside the older man who was probably Daly's trainer or manager.

"No shit, Daly is one lucky bastard," Nico said, and I glanced over at him.

"You think the man beside him is O'Hagan?" I asked and turned back to the ring where the fighters bumped fists and stepped back to wait for the referee to give them the go ahead. The referee's arm dropped between them, and the fight began.

"Yeah, has to be O'Hagan. Holy shit, Daly's quick. That right arm punch would have hurt like a bitch if Matvi had landed it," Nico said as we both leaned forward and placed our elbows on our knees and focused on the fight.

The crowd around us got a little rowdy as they shouted for the fighter they wanted to win. Matvi seemed to have the largest following present with his name being chanted every time he landed a blow or kick.

Daly wasn't to be counted out as he sidestepped a punch only to counter it with a kick that had his ankle and foot making contact with Matvi's right side around his kidney. The grunt and twinge to the side showed the blow had some power behind it.

Matvi went for Daly and tried a grappling hold for a takedown, but Daly was ready for the move. Before Matvi got close enough, Daly stepped back, performed a roundhouse kick that Matvi couldn't get away from, and it landed on the left side of

19

Matvi's ribs. The bell sounded, and round one ended, saving Matvi. He walked to where Christoph Kiev, owner/trainer of Kiev's Gym waited. Kiev was the current heavyweight belt holder. While Matvi drank water, I noticed Christoph talked and another guy wiped his face down and then pressed his fingers up and down his sides, checking to see if Daly's kicks had broken any ribs.

Christoph pointed to the other side of the ring, and Matvi looked briefly to his opponent's corner. When I glanced toward Shawn Daly's corner, the woman was wiping a cut on his brow and talking with Daly. O'Hagan stood beside them, nodding in agreement.

"Well, that's new. O'Hagan isn't even giving Daly any advice. The girlfriend's talking with Daly," I said, squinted, and wished I could have heard what was being said.

"If he's trained him right, Daly should know what to do. Daly is not saying anything at all, he is nodding his head along with O'Hagan. Right there is why your woman should sit in the stands with everyone else. She's probably nagging him about where they are going after the fight," Nico said and shook his head. I chuckled because yeah, Nico was probably right. The woman was a looker, and even though the t-shirt hit mid-thigh and was a little loose on her, it did nothing to hide the curves underneath.

Round two started and Daly came out ready. It showed then that O'Hagan had coached him well.

20

No way would the fight go all three rounds. Matvi was barely hanging on with two minutes left in the second round. Daly charged Matvi low, wrapped his arms around his thighs, lifted, and the two men toppled to the mat with Daly on top. He straddled Matvi to where the only thing he could do was block the punches Daly tried to land on his face while Matvi tried to buck Daly off.

Matvi hips lifted and dislodged Daly, but he wasn't quick enough to turn the tables on Daly. Both men got back to their feet, moved in, and tried to land a punch on the other.

The entire place was on their feet. I could tell the fight wasn't going to last the whole round. The two fighters broke apart, and Matvi seemed to get a second wind as he set up his next move. Instead of going forward, he moved back, and I watched as his hips turned and he kicked out and up, going for Daly's chin. The crowd around us yelled for Matvi. However, Daly caught Matvi's leg before it landed, then Daly held onto Matvi's leg, swung his right leg out, and twisted his hips. Daly brought the leg forward and when it landed, hitting the side of Matvi's head—Matvi crumbled to the mat, out cold.

"Son-of-a-bitch that was one helluva move," Nico yelled over the crowd.

"No shit. This fight is going to help Daly advance. Matvi was pretty much guaranteed a shot at the welterweight belt after a few more wins on the circuit. Not now after this loss to a relatively unknown," I said as the referee raised Daly's arm in show of the win. Then Daly turned and picked up his girlfriend and swung her around before he set her back on her feet and shook O'Hagan's hand before the three left the ring. After the ring was empty, the mat was wiped of any blood and sweat in preparation for the next fight.

Nico and I watched the middleweight, light heavyweight, and heavyweight matches, but they didn't come close to the action that took place during the welterweight matchup. Each fighter who competed throughout the day had come from a different gym in the area.

By the time we headed to the parking lot, our minds were made up. We knew precisely which gym we wanted to be a part of. It would be up to the gym and trainer if they would take us on.

# Chapter Two

## Nico

I pulled the truck in the lot beside the building and parked. Max and I got out and headed toward the entrance. It had been two weeks since Max and I made the decision to go by O'Hagan's Gym. Work had kept us busy and had left little time for anything extra. The job had taken everyone working fourteen days straight to get the build back on schedule. And though the MMA was important to us, we would never place our families' livelihood at risk by leaving them in a lurch.

"For seven o'clock on a Saturday morning, the lot has quite a few vehicles," Max said as we walked toward the entrance.

"Hope O'Hagan is here, and it's not just guys getting in a workout." I stopped and bent to tie the shoestring of my work boot. Max and I decided yesterday we would stop in and check out the gym on our way to the job site.

"Me, too. If all goes well, maybe we can get started next week. By then, we should be able to work out every day. We only have the shingles to lay on the roof to have that part finished. Dad said the brick crew was scheduled to be done at the other build by week's end," Max said as I stood, then we continued to walk.

M&A Construction ran four main work crews, it enabled us to have several builds going at the same time. We also had specialty crews: bricklayers, plumbers, electricians, finishers. There was nothing on a job that had to be subbed out.

When we opened the door and stepped inside, the sounds and smells that greeted us were ones of familiarity: grunts from a punch landing on its intended spot, the hum of a bag caused by the repetition of hits, curses, yelling, and the aroma of sweat that exists in the air after men have pushed their bodies to the limit and sometimes beyond.

"Shit, more guys here than the parking lot showed," Max said as we walked in, stopped, and looked around.

The gym was good sized. It had an open floor, ring in the center, mats off to each side, free weights off to the right in the back corner area, on the left were several different bags set up. There was a large doorway in the back, which looked to lead into a hallway. The gym showed its age by the look of the walls and the flooring, which was scuffed and scarred.

"The place could use a facelift," I said as I continued to look around.

"Maybe a little. Some paint on the walls, a new floor. I like how it is though. This is a working gym, not some spa. I bet this place holds a lot of history." Max turned to look at me, and I nodded in agreement.

"Hey, there's O'Hagan on the other side of the ring," I said and gestured in the direction where the man stood and watched the two men in the ring sparring.

"Looks like," Max said, and I followed as he started to walk to where O'Hagan was. We reached the side of the ring, stood back, and watched while we waited for him to finish with the guys in the ring.

"Switch it up, Malone. You're leading with the right every damn time!" O'Hagan yelled at one of the men in the ring. Both men had to have been going at it for a while if the perspiration on their bodies was any indication.

Max and I watched the two men exchange punches. One man wore black shorts and the other red. The one in the red I would guess was the more seasoned by the skill he showed as he blocked the other man's attempt to land a punch.

"Alright, boys, break it up," O'Hagan said, and the two men broke apart as another man stepped in the ring to help them pull off their gloves. After the gloves had been removed, the man handed each one a bottle of water and a towel. They stood in front of O'Hagan as he continued to talk while they wiped themselves down and rehydrated. "Not bad for a morning workout. We got three months, Comer, until your first fight, and four before you are up, Malone," O'Hagan pointed at the guy in the black shorts, "Malone, you've got to break using that lead in move. Son, it won't take long for your opponent to key in, and when he does, it will be one quick fight because you leave your chin wide open every single time. One perfectly placed uppercut and you will be down for the count. Now give me twenty minutes on the bags, and then you can hit the showers."

Max and I watched the fighters step through the ropes and head across to where the bags were. Mr. O'Hagan spoke to the helper and then turned around and noticed Max and me for the first time since we entered the gym.

"What can I do for you, boys?" he asked as his brows creased while he looked us both up and down. I was sure it had to do with the fact we were dressed in our work clothes.

"Sir, we are MMA fighters," I pointed between Max and me, "looking for a gym to take us on. I'm Nicolo Asaro, and this is my cousin, Maximum Masetti." I stuck my hand out and he shook it, then Max did the same.

"I'm Kearney O'Hagan, the owner. Sorry, I've not heard of you boys. Besides needing a gym, what makes you think O'Hagan would be a fit for you?" he asked and looked between Max and me.

26

"We watched Daly fight Matvi Crav at the United Center a couple weeks ago. Crav is good, your boy is better. We liked what we saw. So here we are." Max was the conversationalist in our family.

"Mr. O'Hagan, we've been training on our own and fighting in local tournaments for the last two years. We've won ninety-six percent of the fights in our weight classes, but without backing, we'll never make it into the circuit." It was quiet for a minute after I spoke as he studied us.

"You're a light heavyweight," he said to me, then pointed at Max, "and you are a heavyweight. We've not been certified yet, so we don't get the breaks like some of the other gyms. I won't sell out to get them either, so if you are looking for that easy way in, you've come to the wrong place."

"We're not, sir. We just want the shot of being the best, and we have no problem working hard to get there." I could tell by Max's tone that he was getting a little annoyed.

"By the way you're dressed, I'd guess you work construction. How do you expect to train if you are working from sunup to sundown?" Mr. O'Hagan turned his head, and I followed the direction to see Daly's girlfriend walking out from the back. Damn and double damn, the woman had on tight red shorts with black around the waist and a black tank top that didn't quite reach the top of the shorts. Max elbowed me and I knew he'd seen her, too. Her red hair was pulled back in a ponytail, which

27

hung halfway down her back. I could imagine what it would be like to grab her hip with one hand, her hair with the other, while she was bent over with my dick buried deep inside her. At that moment, Daly being a lucky bastard crossed my mind again as I watched her walk in our direction. She looked at us, then turned to the corner where the two from earlier had finished with the bags. She stopped to talk with them, and I shook my head to clear her out before I turned my focus back to O'Hagan.

"We work for M&A Construction, it's our families' business. Fortunately for us, our families understand our desire in doing this and back us. We'll be able to put in the hours needed and still be able to work with them. And if this all works out," I waved my hand around, "well, we'll be committed to seeing it through no matter what it takes." After I had finished, I waited to see what else he was going to question, but Max jumped back into the conversation.

"We don't want to waste your time, Mr. O'Hagan. Do you have a heavyweight and a light heavyweight already training here? Is that your reluctance even giving us a chance? I'd welcome someone in my weight class to spar with," Max pointed out.

"No, not at this time.," Mr. O'Hagan answered.

"The two sparring when we came in, they aren't MMA bound?" I asked and caught movement out of the corner of my eye. The

28

woman was headed our way.

"No, they are strictly boxers. I oversee them, and Teagan oversees the MMA side." Mr. O'Hagan turned when he finished and smiled at the woman who walked up.

"Is Teagan the trainer, too? We were under the impression you were the manager. You were the only one ring side at Daly's fight. Except for his girlfriend," I mentioned, and the woman turned to look at Max and me.

"Yes, you were ring side that day," Max piped in, and Mr. O'Hagan chuckled while Daly's girlfriend looked between us, then her mouth curved up on one side.

"I'm Teagan, and you are?" What the woman said took a second to register. Of course, Max didn't seem to suffer with processing what she said.

"Daly's girlfriend is your trainer?" Max blurted out.

"Excuse me," Teagan's eyebrows furrowed as she spoke. With the tone used with the two words, Max and I might have assumed too much. Before I could make a comment, Max, who hadn't picked up on her tone, continued.

"I don't care if you and Daly are an item. What I do care about is you being the trainer. You're a girl for fuck's sake. What are you going to teach me about fighting and taking down an opponent," Max said and looked her up and down. As family, I loved Max, but one thing he didn't possess was a filter. If

29

he thought it, he voiced it.

I watched Teagan's eyes change, darken in color from the pale green I'd noticed when she first walked up. Her face grew a little flushed, and I didn't think it had anything to do with being embarrassed.

"You don't think a female can be a trainer? You sexist asshole. Let me inform you, I'm not a girl, I'm a woman, and you have some serious issues if you can't tell the difference." She crossed her arms over her chest, bringing attention to her chest, because yeah, I looked there, and she stared at Max.

I shifted my eyes to Mr. O'Hagan, who seemed to be doing everything in his power not to laugh, as he watched his trainer and Max have a stare down. Why I felt I needed to intervene was something I would analyze later. But someone needed to take control of the situation before our chances of O'Hagan's Gym supporting us slipped away and we hadn't even received it to begin with.

"It's not so much that you're a gir...I mean woman, but how does Daly like his girlfriend working every day with a bunch of guys, getting groped for the sake of training?" Green eyes cut to me, and I was sure if I looked closely, I would have seen smoke coming out of her flared nostrils. But nope, there laid another issue I would think about later. Her attempt at a death glare turned me on and my work pants got a little tighter to the point I needed to reach down and adjust the crotch.

"Teagan? They came in to see if the gym would be willing to let them train here," Mr. O'Hagan said and drew her attention away from Max and me.

"You have got to be kidding me. Seriously, Dad, why the hell would I want to take on two Neanderthals? They—"

My eyes widened, and I looked at Mr. O'Hagan. I might not have spoken out loud, however, I wanted it put on the record that I was smarter than Max. Only good thing to come out of it was my hard-on deflated.

"Oh hell no. You're his daughter *and* Daly's woman? What kind of qualifications do you have to be a trainer?" With Max's raised voice, heads turned, and men stopped working out. I wasn't looking forward to showing up at the job site beat all to hell.

"Get over the girlfriend shit, asshole. I could show you my qualifications in under five minutes in the damn ring." Teagan looked Max up and down, "Want to try that, big boy?"

"What? You want to spar with me? Sweetheart, I got like eight inches in height and probably about," Max ran his eyes down her body and back up, "a hundred and thirty pounds on you. Under five minutes? I could have your ass pinned in under five seconds." Max's words officially validated that I was the smart one, and we would be in search of another gym.

"Okay, enough," Mr. O'Hagan finally spoke, shaking his head with a smirk on his face. "Teagan, it *is* your decision whether we take them on. I do think you should at least see what they can do before you make your mind up. Schedule them to come in and spar with a couple of the guys. They look like they're headed to work."

Teagan faced her dad, and I elbowed Max and frowned at him when he turned toward me. He cocked an eyebrow and shrugged his shoulders, then he smirked.

Goddammit, he was already over his mad. I'd always envied that about him and when he cut his eyes to Teagan and then back to me, I knew he was interested in her. Max and I shared women often. We enjoyed it. We'd never had a problem finding women who were game enough to take us on for the experience of being with two men, but there never had been one woman whom we both agreed upon. One woman we knew who could handle us both in life, not just for a night. The relationships we had before if you could call them that, didn't last long. The women liked the idea of having two men's attention geared toward them. However, a relationship was more than sex so after the newness wore off, either the woman bolted, or we did. We couldn't seem to find the right one.

"We can do it now. It isn't like it will take long." Teagan looked directly at Max.

"We need to get to work. I'll leave our cell numbers so you can call us when you set up a time," I said to Mr. O'Hagan.

"Teagan, set a time up. Daly should be here

soon anyway," Mr. O'Hagan said, and Teagan stopped the stare off with Max and faced her dad.

"Now. We got time. Do you have any workout shorts? If you don't, I'm sure one of the guys have an extra pair you can borrow," she sneered at Max.

"Sweetheart, there won't be any sparring going on because it will be handled that quick. But I'll indulge you. Set a time." Max smiled at her, and she glared back. I wanted to laugh at the absurdity of it all.

"Mr. O'Hagan, are you really going to let your daughter get in the ring with him?" Surely the man would bring the situation back to some semblance of normal. He wouldn't want to take a chance his daughter would get hurt. Though Max would never intentionally hurt a woman, Mr. O'Hagan didn't know that.

"If you boys are going to last around here, you might want to remember that it is...," he pointed to Teagan, "...her way or no way."

I got a bad feeling when I looked around, and every man in the place stood close to us. The smirks on their faces didn't help either.

"Are you scared I'm going to hurt your manly pride?" Teagan taunted.

"The hell with it. It's on, sweetheart, find me some shorts. We can be late to the site." Max looked at me, "At the very least, I'll get to start my day by rubbing up against a beautiful woman for a few minutes."

I shut my eyes, pinched the bridge of my nose

with my two fingers, and inwardly groaned. I hadn't missed Mr. O'Hagan's comment about us lasting around there, and now, we were more than likely going to have to find another gym. That's if we got out of the place without our asses being handed to us by Teagan's father because of the comment Max made. I dropped my hand and opened my eyes when laughter came from the men who surrounded us. I cut my eyes to Mr. O'Hagan, and he smirked.

"Well, someone get the man some shorts. At the very least this ought to be interesting," O'Hagan said and then of all things, slapped Max on the back. "Call me Kearney…," he looked between us, "…because if you survive the next five minutes, we'll be seeing a lot of each other." He grabbed his daughter's arm and pulled her over to the ring. While they whispered to each other the guy named Malone, who was boxing when we entered, told us to follow him. He had shorts in the locker room Max should be able to fit in.

On the way there, I wondered if we hadn't been set up. Just fucking great.

# Chapter Three

## Teagan

What the hell? I'd been in the back on a phone call trying to set up a sanctioned fight for Shawn, and then headed out to give my dad the good news when I saw them. It caught me so off guard that when I saw Malone and Comer at the bags, I veered toward them. I watched from the corner of my eye as the men spoke to my dad and inwardly chastised myself for being a big chicken. They were similar in build with one just slightly taller than the other. They each had dark brown hair, one was cut short while the other's was a little longer and curled at the ends. Their skin was olive and combined with the dark brown eyes, they were absolutely the most gorgeous men I had ever seen. And it wasn't like I never saw good looking men before. I'd been around them almost my entire life at the gym. Not once in all the time I spent around men had I ever felt a warmth run through my blood from just the sight of one. And it happened in one night with two different men. What are the odds of that? It made my reaction toward them irritate me more than a little.

After a few minutes had passed talking with Malone and Comer, I steeled my back and headed to my original destination of where my dad was. No way was I going to let two hot guys stop me.

As I got closer to my dad, I picked up their conversation and their interest in the gym. At least until they spoke to me, especially the bigger of the two. Every word that left his mouth had my temper going up a degree. The whole situation was what brought me to my current spot by the ring with my dad as the men followed Malone to the locker room.

"Teagan, what is going on? I know your temper gets the best of you sometimes when the guys start in on you being a woman, but you never acted like that before." My dad was a perceptive man, however, it didn't mean I would break down and give him the real issue I had with them.

"He was an asshole about me being a woman trainer. Which was bad enough, but he had to make the insult even worse by calling me a girl. It's like he thinks that because I'm female, it makes me less knowledgeable about the sport or makes me lack the ability to see weaknesses," I snarled, then sighed and looked up at my dad. He wore an expression I had never seen before. "What? You can't be worried I am going to get hurt sparring the big one?"

"Of course not. The opposite actually," Kearney O'Hagan said while he signaled at Jonesy, who helped out around the gym, for a pair of gloves.

"Seriously, what is going on? The guy says he is going to rub up against me and you, my father, the man who purposely held late evening workouts for the boxers when I was in high school and out on a date. The same man who, just a month ago, donned gloves and put on a show in the ring at the same time I walked in with my date." I held my hands out to him, and he placed the gloves on and chuckled to himself.

"Give your old man credit. I remembered the names of those two. Are they not the men you spoke about when you came from that amateur tournament at the Hammond Civic Center a bit ago? Wasn't it you who said they were good and could be better with a little work? And they possessed more raw talent then you've seen in a while."

"So, a lot of the amateurs have skills." I shrugged.

"They will be good additions to the gym. If we get sanctioned in, Teagan, we'll have half the weight classes covered."

"They are cocky and pissed me off," I sighed.

"They have values. They work in the family business."

"Oh my God, did you grill them?" The man had no shame.

"No."

"Milton works with family and—" I stopped talking mid-sentence when he started laughing.

"Milton eyes got so huge when he saw me in the ring," he said through his laughter.

"Yeah, because when you saw us come in you swung and it caught Travis off guard and knocked him on his ass." I put my hand up to stop him from interrupting me again, "And then leaned over him and yelled that if he ever looked at me cross-eyed again you would beat him to a pulp." I cocked my brow at him.

"I raised you to be a strong woman. You need a strong man by your side. You should be thankful I saved you from wasting any more time on him. He is a spoiled young man."

"He is a nice man with a very good job. He is VP of Marketing for Soloman Industries."

"Please, that is a title his father gave him in his company. You need a man who can protect you, not one worried about getting dirt under his nails. I don't trust men with soft hands. Besides, who names their kid Milton anyway? That is a pussy's name." He held the ropes apart, and I entered the ring.

"Dad!"

"What? You're around enough men that nothing should shock you. Anyway, I am the parent." I snickered and moved to the middle of

38

the ring. "Don't you laugh at me, lassie. I'll turn you over my knee." I turned around and looked at him. He had his arms crossed over his chest as he glared at me.

I snorted, "Yeah, sure. How many times have you done that? Oh wait—never."

He looked past me toward the back. "Ah, here they come," he said, and I turned to watch as the men walked out from the back. My temper had left, but now it was easing its way back along with the same warmth I'd felt in my stomach from the first time I'd seen them. What was it about them? Yes, I'm a woman who appreciates a hot body so when Nico had his fight and my belly flipped as I checked him over, no big deal. But then, Max took the ring, and everything I felt for Nico happened again. Two men. Really? My body picked that night to act extra female. It'd been the main reason I'd put off getting in contact with them, and now here they were.

"Well, I'm ready. How about you, sweetheart? What's classified as a takedown? I don't want to hurt you," Max said as Nico held the ropes apart for him. I looked around, and every man in the gym had moved ringside to watch.

"Pinned for a count of ten." My eyes traveled to his chest, his nipples were pierced, the silver loops shining from the lights. Tattoo tribal markings wrapped both shoulders. Other than that, his skin was smooth with no hair until you reached the dark smidgen that led and disappeared into the waistband of his shorts. "Those will be painful if they get ripped out." The look I received for my response was the slow curve upward of his lip and a cocked eyebrow.

"I take them out for fights. You have any metal on you, sweetheart?" When he stared into my eyes, a shiver went through my body, one I hoped was only on the inside and not on display for all to see. I had no doubt the man was dangerous to all females. If he made it onto the circuit, every fight there would be panties offered with phone numbers written on them from women who were looking for the chance to tell their friends they got nailed by whichever fighter took them up on their offer. Or worse, the ones out for the payday being successful in the MMA brings.

"You two ready?" We broke eye contact when my dad spoke, and I turned to nod at him. "Okay, five minutes or the ten-count pin. Give Nico the watch Malone, he can keep track of the time and I'll act as the referee."

My eyes cut to Nico and his slow smile told me that he caught the play between Max and me. His wink more or less confirmed it. I glared at him, and he chuckled. No doubt Nico was just as dangerous to women as Max was. Nico held his hand out and accepted the watch from Malone. We waited until he had the stopwatch in hand and then my dad moved to our sides putting his arm out between us. When his arm dropped, the countdown began.

I stepped back and to the side as Max lunged

for me, his arms wide open only to grab air. His forward momentum cost him as I kicked out and made contact with the back of his leg, he stumbled. Max's balance was good and it impressed me when he was able to recover his balance instead of falling to his knees. He turned toward me, and I was ready. I kicked my leg up and out to the side and caught him in the chest. To my surprise, he was ready and had taken his own step back, which kept the blow from being full force when it landed.

He was on me before my foot was back on the mat and I was able to brace myself. He came at me low, wrapped his arms around my thighs and lifted me off the ground. The grappling move should have put me on my back with Max landing on top of me, but instead, he fell back to the mat bringing me down on top of him. He never made a sound as his body hit with my added weight. I knew what he planned to do, yet I paused, the feel of his body under me was a distraction, one I did not need right then.

"Watch the roll." I heard Travis's voice and realized that Max was lifting his hips with his arms still wrapped around me. I raised up, using his chest to push off, which caused him to release me and then I scrambled off before he could flip us. If I allowed him to get his weight on top of me, I knew it would be over.

"Ah, sweetheart, I liked that position." I started to pant as we moved around each other looking for an opening and the sad part was, it

41

wasn't from the exertion. Max wasn't even trying to catch his breath, and I felt like my lungs were on fire, which made me mad. I was letting him get to me. I, of all people, knew what happened when you lost focus.

"Well, you should have stayed down." His chuckle made me even madder, and I swung my body around as if to kick out. He moved in just like I thought he would, but instead of kicking out, I dropped down, swept my leg out across the mat and took his feet out from under him. As Max fell forward, I scrambled out of his way. He caught himself with his hands, and I was up and straddling his back before he raised himself to his feet. The move had Max hitting the mat instead.

"Sweetheart, you seem to like being on top. I'm all for that, but it would be better if I were on my back with you straddling me," Max said, bucked, and pushed off the mat as if my weight on top of him was nothing. I slid to the mat and landed on my butt. I jumped up just as he turned around to face me.

"Two minutes left!" Nico yelled from his position.

"Teagan, why are you playing with the young man?" my dad asked, and I cut my eyes toward him, and he smiled. The man had lost his mind.

"Don't stop, I like you playing with me," Max said and moved toward me. I had had enough of the innuendos, so I turned sideways, prepared to swing my leg back and then forward and up to

42

catch him upside his head, but the asshole was ready for that move. "Did Daly teach you that or did you teach it to him?" he asked and in a series of fluid movements, he dropped my leg, wrapped me up in his arms, and threw his weight into me, and both of us headed toward the mat. Unfortunately, it was with me underneath him this time.

I would swear later that time slowed as we took the tumble because I waited for the blow to my back as it made contact with the mat. Max's added weight, well that, I expected to hurt like a bitch while it robbed me of my ability to breathe. The impact was going to knock the breath right out of my lungs. I closed my eyes in anticipation of the pain, and maybe a hospital visit, along with berating myself for letting my temper get the best of me and challenging the baboon.

The 'oohs' and thud sound had registered before I hit the mat. I felt a little heaviness on top of me but nothing like what I expected. I opened my eyes and got the answer to why I wasn't flattened like a pancake. Max had taken the fall, and most of his weight rested on his forearms as they laid on each side of me. He had even placed his hands were under my head, which kept my head from making direct contact with the mat.

"You okay, sweetheart?" Max whispered as he looked down at me.

Was he serious? He hadn't completed the takedown. Something a fighter should never do was give his opponent the slightest of openings.

I looked him in the eyes, bent my legs up until my feet were planted flat on the mat and rolled my hips from side to side. With my hands on the mat already, I arched up to push him off. His eyes widened as the guys around us cheered me on. I smiled and continued to roll from side to side, the added advantage of being smaller.

I hadn't gotten to enjoy Max's surprise in my move before he pushed his lower body into me, removed his hands from behind my head, laid the rest of his body down until we were chest to chest, then grabbed my arms and placed them over my head. He bent his head down to the side of mine, and his warm breath at my ear made me shudder.

"Now this is my favorite position," Max whispered in my ear, then I felt the tip of his tongue circle my ear. Startled, I whipped my head to face him. "Sonofabitch!" he yelled while pain shot through my chin when it made contact with his cheekbone.

I gave one last ditch effort to move as I wiggled under him and immediately stopped when the movement aligned us perfectly, and his cock pressed down on my pubic bone. His size was impressive, the thin material of our shorts disguising nothing underneath it. I bit back a moan before it escaped my lips.

"Time!" was yelled by Nico at the same time as my dad's "Ten!" registered in my brain.

By the time everything hit me, Max was gone. My arms were free along with the weight of his

44

body. I laid there as my dad approached and leaned over me.

"Well, Teagan, what do you think?" I looked at my dad, shook my head, rolled over, and pushed up off the mat. The guys who had watched were now passing money between each other while Max and Nico stood in one of the corners. Max drank from a bottle of water someone must have given him as both men watched me.

I walked to the ropes, stepped through, and headed toward the office in the back. I had to be out of my mind. I no longer could deny the effect the two men had on me, but for the good of the gym and the men who represented it, I yelled over my shoulder, "See both of you Monday. Five thirty, and that is in the morning. Nico, I'll evaluate you then." I kept walking and rolled my eyes when I heard my dad welcome them aboard.

"That's all you're going to say?" Max asked loudly.

"Nope. You need to work on your speed," I answered as I reached the doorway that led to the back.

"Took you down, didn't I, sweetheart?"

"I'm a girl, remember?" I shot back.

The laughter followed me until I reached the office and closed the door, then let the smile spread across my face. I was so screwed.

# Chapter Four

## Max

"You're going to catch so much shit at the job," Nico said and continued to laugh. The fucker had been laughing since we left the gym.

"It's only a small bruise on my cheek. Shut up, dickhead."

"What the hell did you say to her that had her head-butting you? I want to know, because if we are going to do this, I don't want to make the same mistake," Nico said, then finally stopped laughing and paid attention to the traffic.

It didn't matter that it was Saturday, traffic around the Chicago area was heavy, no one day more special than the other. It seemed people always had somewhere they needed to be.

When we reached the job site, loads of activity greeted us. It looked like the brick laying crew had started on the outside, but then, I noticed several

47

of the men, who should have been working on the inside, stood off to the side talking with my brothers and Nico's brothers. Even the brothers-in-law were involved.

"That answers a lot," Nico said as we started toward the group of men. I turned and followed to where he was looking.

"Holy shit," was blurted before the thought had even finished registering.

"I know, right? Have to say that beats last week when we were up on the roof, and she was laying out by her pool topless," Nico said as we stopped by the group of men.

"You got to wonder if the husband knows," Colton, my cousin, and Nico's oldest brother, said but never took his eyes off the woman next door.

"What are you doing here? Why aren't you at the other build with the crew?" I asked my brother, Joe, who was in the group of men, too.

"Dad and I swapped out today. I might add that you assholes have been holding out. At the other build, the lady next door is an old bitty who comes out at least once a day to scream at us for something. Either we are too loud or by that, I mean because you know the nail gun has a volume button." Everyone laughed as Joe continued. "Christ, last week the cops showed up. The woman had called them and said a few of the men were peeking in her bedroom window."

I looked at Joe. "Seriously, who was it?"

"It was Walt, Sam, and Tate. They weren't

looking in her window; they were up on the damn ladders putting the siding on. That's the build with the siding on the top half, brick on the bottom," Joe informed but never once looked away from the woman next door. I grinned and was glad at the same time Joe was the one dealing with the other build.

"Yeah, the one the young woman bought and wanted gutted and renovated?" I asked.

"That's the one." Joe finally turned and looked at me.

"Well, what did the cops say?" Nico asked.

"Hell with the cops. What happened to your face?" All heads turned toward me at Joe's question.

"Yeah, Max, tell them what happened," Nico said and burst out laughing. "I told you."

"I thought you two were stopping off at O'Hagan's Gym?" Grayson asked.

"We did," Nico answered his other brother, then frowned at him. "Why are you out here watching the neighbor?"

"I'm bi, bro. You suddenly got a problem with that? Besides, there is nothing wrong with my eyes, dumbass. I can appreciate an excellent body," Grayson fired back, and I snorted. I loved family.

"Can Evan?" Nico asked Grayson.

"Why you so interested in my partner, bro?" Grayson questioned.

"Because..." Nico didn't finish what he was going to say.

49

"Can I what?" Evan asked as he approached. Grayson smacked Nico on the back of the head, then lifted his chin in the direction of the lady's house, and Evan followed his lead.

"She the one you said laid out with no top?" Evan questioned as he stared across at the woman.

"That would be her," Grayson commented.

"I'd do her, she's hot as hell. Best of both worlds. Doing her while you do me." Grayson laughed at Evan's words and the rest of us groaned. The groan wasn't because of their sexual preferences, no one gave a rat's ass, it was more not wanting the details.

"That is what I say. Well, not the part about being bi. Just the part about nothing being wrong with my eyesight." I stared at my one and only brother-in-law, Corbin.

"Dude, if Marianna catches you out here, you are on your own. Nice knowing you, too, and I promise to say something nice over your grave." My sister worked on the crew that laid the sheet rock and prepared the ceilings and walls for the painters. She was scary as hell when she got mad.

"She's not here today," Corbin answered.

"Then why are you here? I thought you were installing the plumbing at the other site?"

"Starts tomorrow. Mari wanted me to stop by and ask if you would watch Pixie next weekend? Kellie has a cheer competition in Indiana." Nico and I both groaned.

"I love my niece, Corbin, but that damn dog is

50

the devil. She hates us. Can't one of you keep her?" I turned and asked Rane and Joe.

"No," they said in unison.

"You suck as brothers, you know that?" I knew I would take the dog, but there wasn't a need for them to know it.

"Yeah, and somehow I can live with that knowledge," Rane said and then we all whipped our heads around when we heard Marcus, one of the men on the bricking crew, cuss. We watched as he tried to wipe the mortar off his hand and arm. Seemed we weren't the only ones distracted by the woman.

"I wish a cold front would come in. If it stays warm, we might have to up our workers' comp," Colton declared, and I had to agree as I watched the lady get down on her knees and then lean forward into the flowerbed.

"Well, hello. Someone gets waxed," Nico said rather loudly, and I elbowed him. The string bikini the woman had on barely covered her very large breasts, and the thong bottom wasn't enough material to cover her other end either.

"Damn, let's go inside. If we don't get some work done today, Dad and Uncle Vinnie will have our hides. Plus, every time she leans in and then back, it's like watching a bird hatching, its little pink beak popping in and out of the shell," Joe asserted and started toward the entrance. With one last look the rest of us followed.

"One pretty bird. Can't wait to see what she

51

does next," Rane said just as we turned the corner of the house.

"Tell Marianna that I'll keep Pixie, Corbin." My hands were bigger than the little Yorkie. However, the dog had no clue she was pint-sized.

"Thanks, Max. We'll bring her and her stuff Friday night," Corbin answered, said his goodbyes and left for the other site. Everyone pitched in and helped with other jobs that needed to be done until the build reached their stage.

We walked into what was to be the living room when it was finished. Nico's brothers and brothers-in-law headed toward the kitchen area. The rest of us stopped at the worktable to look over the plans that were laid out. Joe turned back around to face me.

"I didn't miss the fact you didn't answer the question earlier about your face," Joe brought up, and Nico laughed, the asshole.

"It's just a damn bruise. Not like my whole face is busted up. I got it at the gym." I hated to admit what happened. They never let anything go.

"Go on, Max, tell them about your sparring match with the O'Hagan's trainer," Nico offered, then smiled and cocked his brow at me. I glared back, which had no effect whatsoever on Nico.

"Sparring. You let the guy get that close to you?" Rane asked.

"Not he...a she," Nico shared and walked off as one of the workers yelled for him.

"Nuh uh, bro. A girl. O'Hagan's trainer is a

52

girl?" Joe asked, amusement already showing on his face.

"Is she a looker?" came from Rane. I just glared at my brothers.

"Oh wow, that look says a lot. She must be the linebacker type." Joe laughed when I sneered at him. "It's okay, man."

"She's not built like a football player, Joe. She isn't a fucking stick either so don't go judging what you don't know or have seen. Teagan is sexy as hell. Buff, yet soft in all the right places," I answered through gritted teeth.

"Chill, bro, I wasn't saying anything was wrong with a woman having something to hold onto while you're lovin' them. I've enjoyed time with both, and nothing's better than sinking into a woman's warmth. The skinny ones, you just need to be more inventive. I love all the shapes women come in." Joe winked.

"Same, except the ones that are shaped like dudes," Rane said and did his hands as if to show what he meant. Then he added, "That's Grayson's area," as he leaned over the plans.

Nico walked back into the room shaking his head. "I can't believe we are related. Grayson hears you, cuz, and he is going to kick your ass."

Rane stood and looked at Nico. "What? Why?"

"Making the gay comment about him," Nico answered, and I watched Rane's face change, and he frowned at Nico.

"Asshole, I can't believe you would think I'd

say shit like that about him." Rane turned and pointed at the plans, "That is what I was referring to. The dead space upstairs between the dormer windows on each end of the house and the bedrooms behind them. That is Grayson's area."

Nico started laughing, and Joe slapped our brother's shoulder. "You are so easy, Rane."

"So, you going to look for another gym?" Joe asked.

"Nah, O'Hagan's it is. We start training next week. I'll call Dad tonight and talk to him about working in our spare time. We don't want to leave any of the crews shorthanded."

"You know Dad and Uncle Vincent are going to be cool with it. And we got you and Nico covered, bro. That's what family does." Joe slapped my back.

"Thanks, Joe."

"Christ, are the two of you going to kiss next? I'm going to work before someone breaks out into a dance." Rane walked off, and the rest of us grabbed our tool belts off the table. Joe nodded, then headed toward the back.

"I'm going to miss this shit every day, Nico."

"Me, too," I agreed before I headed toward the temporary stairs. Even though, I would miss working everyday with my brothers and cousins, I was excited for what was to come for myself and Nico.

# Chapter Five

## Nico

It was still dark outside on Monday morning when we walked into O'Hagan's Gym. The lights were on and Teagan came walking out from the back and damn it all to hell did she not have any other workout clothes but the tiny shorts and form fitting sport's bra things? Maybe a t-shirt, jeans, a robe, men's overalls, anything that would cover most of her body.

The whole thing might be harder than what Max and I first thought. We were attracted to her, but we weren't animals. We would control ourselves—maybe—and as long as no one asked our brothers—or Sister Frances, the nun who taught us in the fifth grade, we would be absolutely fine. We were raised to be gentlemen.

"You and I are screwed if she continues to wear those outfits," Max whispered. "It's going to be tough to train with a hard-on."

I didn't answer Max, I only smiled at Teagan when she walked toward us. If we needed to, we could always go up a size in our shorts for the extra room.

"Morning, boys. Glad to see you are on time. You ready for this?" Teagan asked.

"You bet, sweetheart. Ready, willing, and able as the saying goes." There was no doubt in my mind Max spoke of more than training.

"Anyone else train this early?" I asked since we were the only ones there unless some of the guys were in the locker room in the back. Which was highly doubtful with the emptiness of the lot when we pulled in.

"No. I wanted to be able to focus strictly on the two of you. I'd like to get you both set to Daly's workout regimen as soon as possible. Then the three of you can work out together. Shouldn't take longer than a week to get you where you need to be."

"So, we are the only three fighters you have?" I stated.

"Yes, for now."

"You aren't going to get us started, then change your mind, leaving us stuck with scheduled fights and no training/manager or gym behind us." I was glad Max asked the question. It had entered my mind, too. Not only was O'Hagan's taking a chance on us—we were taking a chance on them. Especially since they hadn't received their certification.

"Okay, can we dump our bags in the locker room before we get started?" I asked and lifted the bag in my hand to show her.

"Sure. Take them on back. I will meet you at the bags." While she headed to the bags, Max and I walked to the back. The locker room was clean, just old like the rest of the place. I noticed the gym had everything it needed to deal with the training of fighters and a few extras seemed to be tuck away in the locker room: sauna, whirlpool tub. There was even a room off to the side loaded with medical supplies.

"Do you think there is more to the MMA commission holding off in certifying O'Hagan's? They don't lack for equipment. So other than the building needing a facelift, not sure I understand why they're dragging their feet."

Max sat his bag on the bench and pulled out his clothes to hang on the hook inside.

"Not too sure. I know Mr. O'Hagan said something about needing fighters. Maybe they will come around since with us, there is three now. I'm more worried they will get their certification and drop us." Max shoved the empty bag in the bottom of the locker while I did the same. "Ready?"

"Yeah, let's go see what she has planned for us." I walked toward the door. "We're sticking to our plan, right?" I asked over my shoulder.

"Yes," Max said as I opened the door.

"No second guessing, even with the MMA

57

holding out on clearing the gym?" I wanted to verify that he and I were still on the same page.

"Yes. Though that isn't the plan I thought you were talking about." Max slapped me on the back and chuckled. "I thought you were talking about letting her get used to us and not going at her full steam because she would probably bolt."

I shook my head. "She would and we don't want that to happen. We have all the time in the world. We'll see her almost every day, which means, she will see us. I'm more worried about her dad going off the deep end. I so don't want him kicking our asses. Remember what Mr. Grazia said when he heard us mention O'Hagan's and Teagan when we were at his place Saturday night? He said Kearney O'Hagan doesn't play around when it comes to his daughter. We don't want to rock the boat at the gym," I reminded Max.

"Yeah, I don't either. Let's see how things go. There is something about her, Nico. I knew when I saw her at Daly's fight. I was pissed off she was with him, and I had no reason to feel like that, I didn't know her. Now, I can't let it go, man, and I realize I should."

"What do you mean by that?" I asked at Max's frown.

"Nico, if one of our brothers said what I'm about to. We would laugh our heads off. She's going to be important to our future and I'm not just saying as fighters. I realize that sounds crazy, but it doesn't change the fact I feel that way." Max shook

58

his head as if he would be able to get rid of the thought or the feelings he was having.

I wanted to tell him it would go away, that maybe it was because we were getting a shot to go to the next level. Yet, I didn't waste my breath because frankly, I didn't even believe it myself.

When we walked out from the back, Teagan stood in the bag area with a clipboard in her hand.

"Nico, you on the big bag. Max, you on the speed bag. I want you to do what I call count ups and downs. I will show you." Teagan stepped up to the speed bag. I hadn't even noticed she had put on fingerless gloves. "See, do left, right. Left left, right right. Left left left, right right right. Go up to ten on each hand, then decrease it as you go backward but switch out the hand you lead with. Ten rights, ten lefts, nine rights, nine lefts." She stepped back, picked up her clipboard, and Max moved to stand in front of the speed bag while I moved to the big one. "Okay. Ready?" We both nodded. "Begin."

It felt good to hit the bag, Max and I hadn't worked out in a couple of weeks because of the build. Now we would get the chance daily. I was looking forward to it. I followed Teagan's requested pattern for the repetitions.

"Not bad. Not bad at all," Teagan praised, then wrote on the clipboard. "Next is the weights."

"Are you going to write everything we do down?" Max asked and leaned over her shoulder from behind as one of his hands rested on a shoulder.

"Yes, you might think it stupid, but the balance between everything you do works," she answered without raising her head up from what she was writing.

"Not dumb, sweetheart." Max squeezed her shoulder, and I saw a small smile on her face before she schooled it and lifted her head.

"Teagan, you hit the bag really well yourself. Lots of practice at it?" I asked. I really wanted to know how she started working in the gym. How she learned the ins and outs of boxing and MMA. I wanted to know everything about her. She looked between Max and I as if deciding if she was going to tell us.

"Come over to the lifting area and I will talk while you get started. Some of the others will be arriving soon. I had hoped to have you through the beginning before they did get here. So, one lifts and the other spots. Start out with one hundred pounds and go up twenty after twenty reps. Your max out when you reach four hundred.

"How much do you know about O'Hagan's?" she asked.

"We are aware O'Hagan's is the third generation with your father owning and running it. Four when you take it over," Max shared the only bit about the gym that he and I knew.

Teagan walked toward the lifting area, and we followed as she talked, "If I bore you, I promise not to be offended if you tell me that you've heard enough." She chuckled and a smile lit her face. "Yes, my great-grandfather started this gym when he came to America from Ireland. It was opened only in the evenings after he worked all day doing carpentry. I was told he could fix and build anything. Anyway, he married and had my grandfather who followed him into carpentry and working at the gym with him and so forth as my dad did when he became of age. My dad, though, didn't want to work doing carpentry because he fell in love with boxing. He started boxing at this gym when he was barely able to stand.

"He was an amateur fighter when he met my mother at a movie theater, and he said he knew she was the one for him as soon as he saw her. They married a month later. I was born a few months after their first anniversary. The upstairs of the gym had been a storage area, but my grandfather remodeled it into an apartment, and my dad moved us into it. The place they had been living at was only one bedroom, so with me, they needed more room.

"Are you bored yet? I know I'm giving you more than you probably wanted to know." She seemed embarrassed about opening up to us. Max and I listened as we went through our reps. We had only completed half of them when she stopped.

"No, we want to know everything about you," Max said and the smile she wore while telling us the story was replaced by a frown. I took the

61

expression as she might be a little confused by Max's statement.

"Max meant umm...since we will be a part of O'Hagan's, it's nice to know the history and how the place came to be. Please continue, Teagan, we aren't bored in the least," I said, and her smile returned.

"Okay," she said and sat on the bench across from the one we were using. "My grandfather fixed the apartment because my dad had just started boxing in amateur competitions. With us living upstairs, it kept him from worrying about my mother and me across town. Plus, he could work out whenever he wanted or needed to.

"My mother would bring me down after I got a little bigger and we'd watch my dad train. He said I would clap my hands and gibber jabber while the sparring was going on. He started to win his fights and people took notice, and he got offers to fight some of the better-known fighters who were ranked. He won those fights, too. One day, after several fights, he got the call he'd work so hard for, his chance to fight for the heavyweight title. Of course, he jumped at the opportunity and started training immediately for it. The fight was to be only a short three months away. The fighter who originally was supposed to go up against the champ had crashed skiing and got pretty banged up and he would be unable to fight. My dad was their next choice. They didn't want to cancel the fight altogether because they had spent a ton of money for the venue and advertising.

"I was three then, and one day when my mother needed something from the store, which was just down the street. She was going to take me, but I cried because my dad was in the ring sparring, and I wanted to stay. Since she wasn't going to be gone long, my grandfather volunteered to watch me while she ran her errand.

"My dad said they heard the sirens as they passed the gym but paid no mind to them because everyone was focused on the training. My mother had been crossing the street, heading home and a taxi turned the corner and didn't see her until it was too late. She died later at the hospital from her injuries. Losing her devastated my dad, and though I don't remember much about her, I'm sure I was confused about why she wasn't around."

"Christ, baby, I'm so sorry." I couldn't think of much else to say. I knew it was just her and her dad, but I never knew what happened to her mother. Max and I had finished the reps with the weights and had been sitting on the bench listening to her, and she hadn't even noticed we were done.

"Thank you." She rose and looked at the clock on the wall over the entrance. "If you want to get a drink and relax a couple minutes, next up you'll be practicing a few of the wrestling moves that are used. I want to evaluate your ability to know when and where you should use certain holds or moves." She started to walk toward the back.

"Will you finish telling us about your dad while

we take a break?" Max asked, and Teagan looked between him and I and nodded. I would give anything to know the thoughts running through her head. After filling a couple water bottles, the three of us sat in the metal folding chairs that were near the ring.

"Well, my dad pulled out of the fight. He couldn't keep his focus on it. Then, he made the decision to train boxers instead of competing as one. He said he lost one of his girls and he wasn't willing to lose the other because he was always training. Essentially, he hadn't want to be the parent who pushed his kid off on others. Shortly after, my grandfather turned the gym over to him, and he started to build a different legacy. Over the years, Dad has turned out a few boxers who have gone on to win championships.

"When I got home from school, I would come down to the gym and watch like I had done with my mother. The men accepted me as one of theirs and started teaching me things. The knowledge I gained here, well...I thought I should put it to good use.

"Besides, my dad gave up a lot for me, why wouldn't I want to help around here? He's my family. I only have him and a couple uncles from my mother's side. My uncles never married or had any kids, and my dad doesn't have any brothers or sisters. So... here I am doing something I have loved being a part of since I could barely walk."

"There are plenty of women who compete in

both sports. With your knowledge and ability, why didn't you go into either the MMA or boxing?" I asked. Teagan couldn't be more perfect for Max and me. The more she had talked, the more I wanted to know about her and the closer I felt to her.

"My dad. He would have supported me. Heck, I would have had the best trainer around. I probably could have done well, too. But competing wouldn't have brought me the enjoyment I get out of teaching and showing the skills to others—and for my dad? He didn't get the son to leave the gym's legacy to. He got me. Before either of you ask, no, he has never once mentioned he wished he had a son. It's me. I want to show everyone that O'Hagan's Gym can stand the test of time. Even with a *girl*..." Teagan put emphasis on the word girl and looked at Max and smirked before she continued. "...in charge. Old gyms have a place and need in communities. New technology is great and all, but I like everything old school.

"That's why I am here." Teagan laughed, and the sound made my stomach tighten. I elbowed Max who hadn't said a word. He just sat there and stared at Teagan.

"Sweetheart, you are perfect," Max said after a minute. His words had Teagan staring back at him.

"Not sure that's true. I have flaws like everyone else," she answered.

"Let us take you out," Max blurted. So much

65

for our discussion on taking it slow with her to get a feel in regard to two men sharing her. However, it seemed Max was going to put it all out there. I wasn't sure if I was upset either. We would at least learn if she was interested or disgusted by the idea.

"Umm... I don't go out with the guys from the gym. It keeps seeing each other all the time uncomplicated. Or trying not to act different around each other if it doesn't work out."

"Teagan, there is no reason for it to be complicated. We like you, like what we see in you. We want to take you out to dinner, or the movies. Whatever you want," I explained and waited for her to respond. She looked at us, sucked her lip between her teeth and bit down. Max groaned, and the front of my pants grew increasingly tight.

"I can't," she proclaimed, then pointed to the mat. "Break's over. Time to practice some moves."

"I'm going to get you to change your mind, Teagan," Max boasted, then turned and headed toward the mat, leaving her standing and staring at his back. A minute ticked by, then she turned her head toward me.

"Does he even listen or is he just an asshole? Or am I the lucky one he uses such charm on?" I chuckled at her sarcastic tone and at the way she frowned as she looked over at Max stretching on the mat.

"No, he doesn't listen, and he only acts like that when there is something he wants." Her head jerked back in my direction. "Something we both want," I added, and her eyes widened but she didn't say anything. She just stared at me. "You do understand what we are talking about, right?" I pointed to Max, then to myself as I asked.

"Yes," her answer was said so low I almost missed it. Then it seemed we were going to have to continue the discussion later when the door opened, and Shawn walked in. However, I didn't want to walk away from her without making things perfectly clear to her.

"I want to make sure there is no misunderstanding, so I'm going to say it straight out. The three of us: Max, you, and me. Max and I like to share." I started toward Max and as I passed by her, I ran my hand down her arm and said low enough that she would be the only one to hear. "We will do whatever it takes to get you between us." I never looked back as I walked to the mat. I wanted what I said to sink in.

Max and I would never force a woman to be with us. Even one we wanted as much as we did Teagan. Everything would be up to her. She held the power whether she knew it or not.

# Chapter Six

## Teagan

Nico and Max sparred in the ring while I stood off to the side. I was close enough to see anything they were doing wrong but far enough away not to get caught in the middle of the two men.

The middle of the two men. There laid the issue.

I wasn't naïve. I knew what they wanted. I just didn't know if I could be *that* woman. But I wouldn't lie to myself either, I wanted to be.

Their first day, they put it all out there—and four days later not another word had been said. At least not anything out of their mouths. What was on the verge of driving me insane was the slight touches. The brush of their fingers as they walked by. The warm breath on my neck when they stood behind looking over my shoulder at whatever I held. A hand to my back when one of them would catch me trying to move a piece of equipment or straighten the mats on the floor. The hand touched my back to stop me and then when I would stand, the hand would slowly slide down my back until it reached the top of my butt, then it was lifted away. They acted like they never noticed the goosebumps on my skin that was left in the wake of their touch. No acknowledgment of the shiver that went through my body when one of them purposely touched the bare skin between my tank and waistband.

No, they knew exactly what they were doing. Driving me bat shit fucking crazy.

Working in a gym, I'd grown used to men without shirts, sweat dripping down their arms, chest, and face. There was not a minute of fantasy on my part for one of the men. Why? Because I evidently had been waiting on Nicolo Asaro and Maximum Masetti to walk into O'Hagan's for my hormones to kick into overactive.

The sad part of it all—it had only taken four lousy days. What did that say about me?

"Are you alright, lassie?" I jumped at my dad's voice. "Teagan, your face is flushed and when I walked up you were mumbling about lazy days or something."

"It's nothing. I'm fine," I answered because no way would I mention where my thoughts had been to my dad of all people.

"You don't look fine. You aren't acting fine either," he pointed out.

"Really, I'm alright, Dad." My dad looked at me, then to the men who were down on the mat. Max was straddling Nico, and Nico was trying to toss him.

"Are they not doing as well as you hoped?"

*If only.*

"No, they are actually exceeding my expectations. I thought maybe two or three weeks to get them used to the routine where it would become second nature, but they pretty much have it down. Next week I think I'll have them work out at the same time as Shawn. It will be nice for them. They will be able to switch out with each other. Give each someone new they aren't used to."

"Max and Nico have worked together; they know what each other is capable of, their limits. That helps but can also hurt if they get comfortable. You can tell, Teagan, those two boys are close, very close." I looked out of the corner of my eye at my dad, and he was frowning at the men.

"Dad? What is it?" I questioned, and he jerked his head toward me like I'd startled him.

"Teagan, are you interested in one of them?" he asked pointedly.

*What the hell?*

"You know I don't date guys from the gym. Why would you ask that?"

"Because I've never seen you out of sorts, ever. This week I've watched you, and it only happens when you are around either of them. I'm

71

old, Teagan, but I'm still breathing. I remember what it's like to be interested in another individual."

"No. You're reading too much into it. I'm not interested in one of them," I quickly answered. Which it wasn't a lie.

*Okay, kind of. Alright, maybe.*

Nico and Max finished with the takedowns and started working on the exchange of punches and blocks.

"Is it both?" My dad asked in a low voice.

I know my eyes went wide and there was no way to stop them. I cut my eyes around the gym to make sure no one had heard him. Thank God, Max and Nico were focused on each other and too busy blocking punches to pay attention to us.

"Have you lost your mind? Two men? What would make you think that? Seriously?" My voice must have gotten somewhat loud because a few of the men turned to look in our direction. Even Max and Nico stopped and looked over at us and frowned.

"Everything okay, Teagan?" Max asked, then cut his eyes to my dad.

"Yes. Dad and I were having a little disagreement, that's all. You and Nico can go if you're finished. Both of you have done great." Both men looked back and forth between my dad and me.

"Same time tomorrow morning, Teagan?" Nico asked.

"Let's switch up and do afternoon. You can sleep in tomorrow since you worked hard this week. And starting next week, Shawn will join you both." They both wore blank expressions as they walked over to me. My dad stepped back out of the way but watched as they each took a spot on each side of me. They leaned in close and looked at the workout sheet I held. When I looked down at it, I felt the heat rise on my cheeks. The sheet was blank.

*That wasn't good.*

"You didn't write anything down." Max looked at me, and when I turned my face toward him, he looked as if he was fighting not to smile. I turned my head the other way, and Nico looked to be doing the same thing.

"Were we that bad, baby?" Nico placed his hand on my shoulder and Max placed a hand on my neck. My skin felt as if it were on fire, and the need to crawl out of it was strong. I glanced over at my dad, and his eyes twinkled but were focused on the men.

"No, I decided I didn't need to write on the chart today. Both of you seem to have the reps down, and the workouts down pat, so you're ready to move to the next stage. Tomorrow afternoon will be short. You'll only going to work in the ring," I sped through the explanation, so I wasn't surprised to see two sets of eyes staring at me.

"Hmm, that's interesting. We're going to get our stuff and leave. We'll give you that excuse, sweetheart, instead of throwing a bullshit card. Tomorrow," Max said, then gently squeezed my neck and let his fingers trail across my shoulder before he walked away.

"See you tomorrow, Teagan," Nico said as his hand slid off my shoulder and traveled down my arm until it reached my hand, then he squeezed my hand and followed Max to the locker room.

I watched them as they walked away, and it didn't escape me that with every step away from me they took, I felt a little distraught. It was absolutely irrational to not have feelings for both of them, but to feel the loss as they walked away. I shook my head and took a deep cleansing breath, then turned toward my dad.

"Teagan—" I held up my hand and stopped him before he voiced anything else.

"I'm going to go upstairs and cook dinner. I'm not sure I can do this right now," the last part I whispered. My dad held the ropes apart, and I stepped between them. He never spoke a word as I headed toward the back. I was grateful for his understanding. I felt out of sorts and ill-equipped to deal with it right then.

As I walked down the hall to the stairway that led up to my home, I prayed I wouldn't run into Max and Nico leaving the locker room. Luck was on my side for a change, and I made my way up the stairs and into our home.

I stepped into the small foyer, then into the living room. To the left was a hallway, which led to two bedrooms and a shared bathroom. On the right there was a shorter hallway that led to the kitchen, laundry room, half bath, and at the end was my dad's bedroom. The place felt huge at times growing up with just my dad and me. If I was honest, it sometimes felt that way now, too.

Dinner was in the oven when I heard the door open. The casserole had another thirty minutes until it was done. Laundry was caught up, and I had straightened and picked up the living room.

"Smells good, Teagan," my dad said as he walked into the kitchen. I stood at the island in the middle of the room putting a salad together.

"Thanks. It's still early. No one left downstairs?" It wasn't often that we closed early. A few of the men who used the gym worked during the day so at night was the only time they could come in.

"Malone is going to close up for me. I came up early for two things. First, I just got off the phone with the MMA commission."

"Did we get sanctioned in?" I stopped chopping the tomato to listen, and I wasn't sure I wanted to hear what was said if my dad's facial expression was any indication.

"They heard we picked up a couple more fighters and had three weight classes covered. In a nutshell, the commission will grant us sanction status if they make it to the World Championship that is being held at Hammond Civic Center this go-around."

"That is in six months! None of them have even fought one time in a certified MMA fight. Daly is the only one to come close with the fight with Matvi Crav who was ready to move up. Crav's fight was scheduled until his loss to Daly and they dropped Crav. So what? Are they going to let mine walk right on in the door? Yeah, no catch to that." When Dad just stared at me without saying anything, I knew I had it right. "You have got to be fucking kidding me. What's the catch?"

"Three fights, six weeks apart. If they win, they get to go to the championship fights."

"And then what? Win it, then maybe they will give us their seal of approval. That is bullshit, and you know it."

"Teagan, it is a test for you, too. Do you realize the opportunities this could mean for you?"

"Do you realize what could happen if they aren't ready?!" I shouted. More concerned for my fighters than what opportunities would open for me.

"I don't doubt you will have them more than ready. Do you doubt yourself?"

I closed my eyes, thought about the days, hours, minutes that I had spent in the gym to lead up to this moment. The blood, sweat, and tears poured into devouring everything to do with the sport.

*Ready? Was I?*

"I'm ready. The guys will be, too. Tell them we'll do it. Have them set the fights up." When my dad smiled, I knew he already had. I smiled back. "You knew I would go for it?"

"Teagan, you are my daughter. I know you better than anyone does." He got a strange look on his face, "At least for now."

"What do you mean by that, Dad?"

I went to the oven, pulled out the casserole, and took it to the table and set it down. While it cooled for a minute, I finished the salad and waited for my dad to answer.

"Well, that's the second thing I wanted to talk with you about. Nico and Max."

I had been delusional with the thought he would drop it all because I escaped him downstairs.

"Dad, I don't know."

"Give me more credit than that, Teagan, and answer me. Are you attracted to both of those young men?"

I hated to tell him and see the disappointment on his face, but I wouldn't lie to him either.

"Yes," I whispered, not looking at him, so I wouldn't see his disgust.

"Look at me, Teagan." I raised my head as tears formed in my eyes. "Oh, honey. Let's sit down at the table and talk a minute.

Dad picked up the drinks I poured, and I grabbed the salad. We sat at the table, and I dished the food out, serving my dad first.

"Are you embarrassed, Teagan? Is that why you didn't answer me before?"

"Shouldn't I be? I'm attracted to two men. Two

77

men, I've known a whopping week!"

My dad picked up his fork and took a bite of his food like it was any other day and his daughter wasn't spouting off like some ho-bag. When I heard the fork hit his plate, I looked at him, and he smiled. I admit for a brief second, I thought he might have lost his mind.

"I know they are good men who grew up together. Family means a lot, and without their families, I imagine taking time off to train would have been difficult. They're close as brothers, and they even share a home. I want you happy, Teagan, and I don't care if it is one man or two. If you are worried what others think, then you aren't the same girl I raised. No man is prouder of his daughter than I am of you. Whatever you decide, I'm here and on your side. I always will be, honey."

"Umm...Dad, how do you know so much about them?" I asked, and his cheeks turned the slightest shade of pink, then he smiled.

"Your uncles know them and their families. They have for years. The families frequently go to Gratzie's. Gio and Tonio went to school with their mothers and fathers. Even grew up in the same neighborhood."

"They go to Uncle Gio and Uncle Antonio's restaurant? My mother probably knew them, too. Not Nico and Max but the parents. How is that even possible that I hadn't ever seen them before the day at the civic center?" I mused, and my dad shrugged.

"Things happen for a reason. Maybe it wasn't time for you to meet them. If I hadn't gone with my friends to the movies one day, I wouldn't have met your mother. And then I never would have gotten you. I love you, Teagan."

Tears formed in my eyes and dripped down my cheeks as I got up and hugged my dad.

"You're wrong, I think I'm the lucky one to have gotten you as a dad. I love you, too."

We stayed like that for a minute or two, then I pulled away and sat back down so we could eat our dinner.

"I would like to know how the commission received information on us picking up Nico and Max," I wondered out loud as I scooped casserole onto my fork.

"If I had to guess, I would say Kiev. If you fail, Teagan, it will be hard to get other fighters to join O'Hagan's and then he could pursue you harder than he is now. The only thing he has going for him is he holds a belt. Not one of the guys from his gym, who have competed, have made it to the top. His fighters lack discipline. Besides, I think he has his eye on you for personal reasons, too." I stopped eating and stared at my dad. "What? I know things."

*Yes, he did.* It seemed more than I ever gave him credit for.

# Chapter Seven

## Max

I parked the truck, and Nico was laughing before we even got out.

"Shit is not funny. The dog is a pain in the ass. I know why Corbin goes to the cheer competitions, shopping trips to the mall, dance classes, and everything else Marianna and the girls want to do. It's because he doesn't want to stay home with the little demon." Nico laughed harder. "You're only laughing because it wasn't your gloves she got ahold of this morning."

"You can hardly tell where she chewed."

I looked over at him as I opened the hatch on the SUV. We grabbed our bags, and it took everything for Nico to compose himself.

"There are tiny teeth marks all over the damn things. You can't miss them," I groused.

"Would you stop complaining about Pixie and

tell me what we are going to do about Teagan. She knows we want her, and she cut us down. Your bright idea of showing her, instead of going for what we want, wasn't bad because she is ready to crawl out of her skin. She is fighting her feelings. The only flaw with the plan, is while we wait for her to realize we are good for her, we are paying the price with blue balls. I don't know about you, but I am sick of cold showers. The showers don't help by the way, and I'm worried the old adage about 'if you keep touching it, it might fall off' actually could happen. That, or I'm going to get damn blisters on my hand."

If I wasn't sharing the same pain, I might have laughed at Nico.

"Okay, I agree. It's been two weeks since I asked her to go out with us. You've witnessed what I have. She's trying to show indifference toward us but isn't pulling it off well. We were worried about Kearney for nothing, not unless I'm reading him wrong. However, I don't think I am. The other day I threw my arm over her shoulders and walked with her to the office. She opened the door, moved from under my arm, then walked into the office and slammed the door in my face. I stood there and stared at the door for like five minutes until Kearney came down the hall from the opposite direction and slapped me on the back and said not to get discouraged," I informed Nico.

"Okay, so we ask her out again. We'd be golden if she says yes—but if she says no again, I got nothing other than going to the pharmacy and stocking up on Aquaphor to keep the blisters at bay while we wait to see if she breaks," Nico filled me in as we walked toward the entrance.

"What other choice do we have?" I questioned while I adjusted the shoulder strap of my gym bag and held onto the carrier with my other hand. Nico held the door open, and we walked in.

"I don't think we have any," Nico answered.

As we passed through the gym, the comments yelled from the guys already there, started immediately.

"I knew we should have left her at home in the freakin' crate," Nico mumbled as we passed Malone and Comer in the ring.

"Yo, kind of small to be a new sparring partner." Comer laughed at his own joke.

"Nah, that's their date from last night. They have to keep her caged so she doesn't run off," Malone piped in. As we kept walking toward the back, he and Comer kept at it.

"It is going to be a long fucking day," Nico commented, and I agreed.

We walked through the doorway to the back hallway and stopped when we heard Teagan's voice coming from the office.

"What was your end game by doing that? We know our gym's not hurting your business, so why? Was it because I refused the offer to work at your place? Or was it because I wouldn't go out with you? Answer me!" Teagan yelled at whoever was in the office with her and I had a good guess who it was.

"Calm down, Teagan. I can offer you better than an apartment over an old gym."

Teagan verified I was right with the next words she said as I opened the office door.

"Don't touch me, Christoph!"

Entering, I dropped my bag, and sat Pixie's carrier on the floor none too lightly. Both Christoph and Teagan turned when the door hit the wall and Christoph dropped the hand he had on her shoulder.

Before I was able to move further into the room to pull Teagan away from the asshole, he yelled. When I looked down, I saw why. The carrier door had jarred opened, and Pixie's little mouth held onto Christoph's leg.

"Ah, look, your three guard dogs have arrived." He looked at me, "Get this thing off my leg before I kick it away."

I put my hand up to keep Nico from lunging and only because the office space wasn't large, and Teagan might get hurt if we started fighting.

Teagan leaned down and picked up Pixie, who released Christoph as she was lifted. I glared at Christoph and he glared back. The sound of footsteps came from behind us, but I didn't take my eyes off Christoph.

"What the hell is going on in here? I could hear the yelling upstairs," Kearney said as he entered the office.

84

"Nothing, Dad. Mr. Kiev was just leaving." The tone of Teagan's voice had my eyes cutting in her direction.

"It didn't sound like nothing from upstairs." The Kearney O'Hagan who had now stepped fully into the room and stood by Teagan was the one I imagined his opponents saw back in the day—the boxer who wouldn't have a problem knocking your ass out.

Christoph held his hands up, then spoke and showed what an asshole he was. "I'll be waiting when your boys go down, Teagan. I was willing to take your dad on as part of the package. The difference in the offer after this, you won't be a trainer in my gym, you'll only be in my bed."

Nico grabbed hold of me as I lunged at the prick. Pixie hadn't like what she'd heard either because her little body lunged alongside mine and Teagan was forced to tighten her grip on the dog.

I hadn't missed the look on Christoph's face when he saw Pixie move. Maybe the dog wasn't so bad after all.

"Get out. Get out of this gym before *I* kick your ass, Christoph. And you better believe the fighters from O'Hagan's will be in the World Championship bouts. One other thing before you take your ass out of this gym," Teagan leaned in and poked him in the chest before she continued. "I wouldn't sleep with you if you had the last dick on earth and we were going to live an eternity."

It was probably wrong to smile, but damn,

Teagan had a little bit of viper in her. Kearney watched, and though he let his daughter get her say, I noticed his fists were balled at his sides ready to defend her.

Nico elbowed me, and when I turned, he too was struggling not to smile. Christoph hadn't said a word while Teagan had gone off on him. He walked to the door, then turned.

"Enjoy the fights, because after you are humiliated, no one will want to sign with you." No one responded to his dig, so Christoph walked out. Teagan petted Pixie who was snuggled up against Teagan's chest. The lucky dog.

"Teagan?" Kearney said, and she turned to look at him. "Don't listen to him. He doesn't know what he is talking about. Anyone would be lucky to work with you."

"I know, he's a jackass," she replied as she smiled down at Pixie. "Whose sweet baby is this?"

"She belongs to my niece," I answered and would have gave anything in that moment to have her hand caressing me instead of Pixie.

"She is a fierce little thing. Hope she doesn't become ill from biting Kiev. Who knows what he's carrying?" she said and chuckled. It was good to know she didn't let things keep her down.

"I'm going to go work with Malone and Comer unless you need me?" Kearney asked Teagan but looked between Nico and me.

"Okay, I'll see you out there," she told her dad as he started to leave. As he passed by Nico and me, he slapped our shoulders and was gone.

"You really okay, sweetheart?" I had to ask.

"More than okay. Thank you both for letting me handle my own stuff. Means a lot. Ready to get to work?"

"Sure. We need to put our stuff in the locker room first, then we're all yours," I said and watched her eyes snap to us.

*Interesting.*

"Teagan, let us take you out after we finish today," Nico threw it right on out there, and I stood patiently beside him and waited. She looked between us, then down at Pixie.

"What do you think, Pix? Should I take a chance on these two?" Pixie barked and wagged her tail. Her whole body vibrated with the move. "Well, looks like Pix thinks it's a good idea."

*From now on, the dog would be getting steak when she stayed at our house.*

"And it will depend on how well you do today," Teagan quickly added.

"In what?" I asked.

"If you can put Nico and Daly on the mat. I will go out with you." She turned to Nico. "Both of you, unless you let him win on purpose, then it is a no go."

"Let's get to it," I said and started for the door.

"You do know that's together, right? Nico and Daly at the same time."

"Sweetheart, it would hardly seem fair any other way," I boasted and walked out.

*Let her think on that a second.*

# Chapter Eight

## Nico

"Goddamn, get your big ass off us." I laid on the mat beside Shawn, who I hoped was still breathing, with Max sprawled over us. "Jesus, you better check your weight. I swear you've put on fifty more pounds," the wheezing that came out when I spoke couldn't have been a good sign.

Teagan, Kearney, and the others who had been in the gym stood around the mat laughing. I might have been too if I was able to get enough air in my lungs.

"I don't weigh that much more than you, asshole." Max shifted so he could raise off Shawn and me. The move at least let us know Shawn was still alive. He groaned when Max placed an arm on his shoulder to push up.

After Max's weight was gone, I laid there and assessed my body. Everything seemed to be working just fine. I looked over at Shawn, who laid on his back with his eyes closed.

"You doing okay, man?" I quizzed, and Shawn opened his eyes and turned his head toward me.

"I think I know how it feels to get hit by a freight train. When the blood circulates back to my legs, I'll let you know."

Max laughed and stood over us. When he held his hand out, I grabbed hold, and he pulled me to my feet, then we both extended a hand and helped Shawn stand upright.

"Well, since you boys are alive, we can get back to work," Kearney said, then walked away with Malone and Comer behind him.

The others went back to their own workouts. I looked for Teagan and found her standing at the edge of the mat holding Pixie and watching us. When her eyes met mine, she smiled. While Max talked with Shawn, I moved beside Teagan.

"Did you enjoy watching me and Shawn get flattened?" I asked, and she chuckled.

"How often has Max done that to you?"

"Are you talking about his linebacker move?" She nodded, and I continued. "Too many times to count."

"You two have a great relationship. When I was younger, I used to wish for a sister or brother. Someone I could be close to like that," she shared.

"No, you don't. It is a concept that sounds good but in actuality, not so much. If you still want siblings, Max and I have spares, and you are welcome to them."

"Rane is available," Max said as he walked up. "None of my family would mind. Well, maybe my mother, she does seem fond of him. Though, the rest of us don't understand why."

Teagan chuckled, then looked around and asked, "Where'd Shawn go?"

"Home, he said he had a date," Max answered and threw his arm over Teagan's shoulders. "Speaking of dates, I think you have one tonight, too."

"Really, and where would I be going?" Teagan asked with an eyebrow lifted.

"That's a surprise, baby. You just be ready. Max and I will come and pick you up later. Dress for comfort," I responded, then winked.

"Not even a hint? It would make dressing easier. How comfortable? Casual comfortable or yoga pants and a t-shirt comfortable," Teagan said and pushed out her lips in a pout. Max and I were getting a glimpse of a new side of Teagan. Playful and teasing Teagan.

"Come on, walk us to the locker room so we can grab our stuff and Pixie's. My sister and brother-in-law should be getting back, and I don't want to miss them picking up Pixie," Max said, and we headed toward the back.

"Oh, I'm going to miss her. She's so sweet." Teagan petted Pixie, who was eating the attention up, and Max groaned. "Stop it, she is."

"Only toward certain people, sweetheart. She

91

hates every male in our families," Max informed her.

"Not true, Max. She likes Rane," I mentioned and laughed.

"Oh yeah, she loves him." Max laughed, too.

"What did your brother do to her?" Teagan stopped outside the locker room and held Pixie tighter to her.

"Not what he did *to* her. He had a female over, and they got a little hot and heavy in the living room. Rane forgot to put Pixie in her kennel," Max said.

"Max, what difference does that make? Why would he need to put her in a crate when he was home?" Teagan questioned.

"She isn't fond of certain sounds. So...she needs to be in the crate when you plan to get down to business because if there is any noise, she doesn't like it." Teagan's eyes got big at my words, and she looked down at Pixie.

"Oh, you poor baby. Do sex noises set you off?"

"Fuck, they set me off," I proclaimed, and Teagan shook her head.

"What did Pixie do?" Teagan asked.

"Let's just say, Rane has a faint scar on his ass," Max said.

Teagan placed Pixie in her carrier when Max lifted off the floor and sat it down on the bench.

"Well, I better get out of here before one of the other guys come in."

"We'll pick you up at six, Teagan," I told her as turned toward the door.

"Okay. Park around back, there are steps that lead up," she said, then walked out.

Max and I packed our bags, and once we were ready, Max grabbed Pixie's carrier, and we headed out. Both of us more than eager for our date with Teagan.

"Damn, I have to admit when she said pull around back and park, I wasn't expecting this," Max said as he pulled in behind either Kearney's or Teagan's car and parked.

"Me either." We got out and looked up and down the alley that looked more like a driveway for the row of buildings. Each building had living space above it, only noticeable from the back. Double garages were across the alley for each building, too, and a fence ran behind them, the whole length of the alley. It looked like each resident had a gate in the fence that led them to a park. On the other side of the park was a body of water.

"Nice setup back here. Lots of privacy," Max said as we walked up the stairs leading to Teagan and her dad's home. We reached the landing, and the door and landing was under a roof. I pushed the buzzer by the door and we waited.

Only about a minute passed before Kearney swung the door open.

"Hey, boys. Come on in. Teagan isn't quite

ready yet," Kearney said and waved us in, then shut the door behind us. We followed him into the living room. "Have a seat."

It was the first time we had to deal with a parent when we picked a woman up. The ones we had taken out had their own places. When we were younger and just entering the dating pool, parents were the norm, and Max and I had met our fair share. However, it was before we decide that sharing a woman was what we wanted.

"Kearney, who did the work putting this place in. They did a great job from what I can see." Max always scanned the workmanship of every place he entered. Kearney chuckled and had us both looking at him.

"M&A Construction did the renovations and took a storage area and turned it into a home."

"Well, shit. That had to be our grandfathers," I said and stood to walk around the room and check the craftsmanship up close.

"You boys interested in my daughter or are you just looking for a little fun?" I knew any good father, which Kearney was, would ask what our intentions were. We expected it, so when he asked, Max nor I was shocked.

I sat back down and looked at Kearney. "We have no intention of hurting her, Mr. O'Hagan, but with the beginning of any relationship, it takes the parties involved to have a mutual agreement on if it works out or not."

Kearney nodded but had a frown on his face as

if in thought.

Max looked over at me, then back at Kearney. "Is that really what you wanted to know, Mr. O'Hagan? I know you haven't known us long, but like Nico said, we have good intentions. I can't say I won't ever hurt her because let's face it, I say shit now that pisses her off. Pretty sure that won't change. But physically you'll never have to worry about that."

"Boy, I wasn't worried about you physically hurting her. If she didn't beat you to a pulp, you damn well better believe I will."

"Understood," Max and I said at the same time.

"I knew the day you boys walked in the gym things were going to change around here. Then Teagan came out, and I saw the three of you together." He sat back on the couch. "She's all I have. I'm trusting her with both of you."

"We will take care of her, if she'll let us," I said, and Kearney looked toward the doorway. I looked over my shoulder and my mouth dropped open.

Out of the corner of my eye, I saw Max stand and he stared at Teagan, too. His face had to mirror mine. The woman looked good in workout clothes, but the jeans with the tight fitted top cut low, holy hell. Her dark red hair with blond streaks curled all the way down and hung free rather than in her usual ponytail. Every piece of clothing hugged her curves, and we needed to get her out of her father's house because I thought it would be rude to get a hard-on while in the man's living room. Max must have had the same thought.

"Teagan, you look, well, just damn," Max exclaimed, then walked over to her. "You are undoubtedly the most beautiful woman I have ever seen."

The blush rose on her cheeks adding color to her pale skin. She wore little if any make-up. We might have seen her every day for a few weeks, but I felt as if I was seeing her for the first time.

*Really seeing her.*

"Thank you, Max," she said, then looked at me and I realized I hadn't said a word. I cleared my throat.

"Max is right. But I would say gorgeous fits you better." The color on her cheeks deepened.

"Are you ready?" Max asked, and she nodded.

"Well, let's head out. Mr. O'Hagan, I'm not sure what time we will have Teagan home. But we'll take good care of her," I said as I looked back at Kearney. He was watching the three of us. It was the same way he'd done over the weeks when Teagan worked with us. Maybe he saw more than what Max and I had. Teagan was his daughter.

"Teagan, text or call me if you aren't coming home tonight." I was sure to have whiplash and so was Max at Kearney's statement. Then I looked at him, and he looked at me. Yes, there was no mistaking what we heard.

"Dad, you could have bypassed that." Teagan shook her head at Kearney. She walked over to him and kissed his cheek. He whispered in her ear, but it was too low for us to hear. Teagan nodded and then walked toward us.

"Have a good evening," Kearney said.

"You, too," Max said as he led Teagan out.

I held the passenger door open and helped Teagan inside. When I moved in behind her, she slid over toward Max.

As Max headed to the restaurant, I rested my hand on Teagan's thigh and enjoyed the fact I was able to touch her.

*Finally.*

# Chapter Nine

## Max

As we drove to the restaurant, I wanted to lay a hand on Teagan's leg like Nico was doing but I knew if I touched her, I would lose my concentration. When she entered the living room earlier, I told her she was beautiful, but Nico had been right. The word wasn't enough to describe the woman beside me. The connection to her grew every day I spent around her. A lesser man might worry about how fast everything seemed to be advancing, but I welcomed it.

Nico and I had at one time discussed the perfect woman for us. We hadn't had a clue then. Teagan was more than I would have ever imagined.

"They faxed the dates and times for the upcoming bouts," Teagan said. She sat between us with her hands resting in her lap as she fidgeted on the seat. I had a full bench seat put in my SUV for comfort. Being a big man, it was hard squeezing into some of the newer models, and when Nico and I were in the vehicle, available space filled quickly. So every small move Teagan made was felt because our legs rubbed against hers.

"First one is in Boston, right?" Nico asked.

"Yes, the second, if you win, will be in New York and then Vegas for the third. Chicago is holding the World Championship this year instead of Vegas. Some mix-up in the scheduling of events for the timeframe, so Vegas and Chicago switched dates."

"Bet that went over well with Vegas," I commented as I pulled into Gratzie's parking lot. Once I found a spot close to the front, I parked.

"They'll still make bank, but yeah, I bet they won't make that mistake again," Teagan said as she slid across the seat to the opened passenger side door where Nico waited to help her get out.

"Okay, no talking shop the rest of the evening. This is about the three of us getting to know each other better," Nico mentioned as he led Teagan to the entrance.

"Good idea," I agreed and pulled the door open.

"Well, that doesn't leave much to talk about," Teagan commented, then chuckled. "But I would love to hear more about your families."

Teagan and Nico walked in as I held the door open, then followed behind.

"Christ, you've got to be kidding," at Nico's

100

words I looked over Teagan's head and inwardly groaned.

"Damn, Marianna," I complained.

"What? Is something wrong?" Teagan turned around and her brows creased as she looked at me. Then it registered what was probably going through her head.

"It's not an ex or anything if that is what has you frowning. An ex might be bad, this is worse." I looked down at her, and the frown was gone, which made me happy. I hoped it wouldn't return when she found out who was there.

"What could be worse than an ex while you are on a date?" Teagan asked.

"You're going to find out. They spotted us," Nico said, and I looked up to see my brother, Joe, headed right for us.

"Who?" Teagan asked and turned around and investigated the dining area. "That is one large group of people," she whispered as our mothers waved and smiled.

"Well, guess you aren't going to have to hear about our families. You're going to get a firsthand experience." I placed my hand on her shoulder and squeezed.

"Oh my God, all of those people are family members," Teagan blurted and looked over at Nico. I saw the panic on her face and then she ran her hands down her jeans and pulled at the hem of her shirt. "I thought when you pulled up to my uncles' restaurant it was going to be an interesting evening."

"What?!" Nico and I both replied at the same time.

"This is my uncles' place."

"They're the uncles you talked about. Your mother's brothers," it wasn't a question, but she answered.

"Yes."

Nico looked at me, and I shrugged. The evening was going to be interesting if nothing else. And if our families ruined Nico and my chance with Teagan, I would be more than pissed.

"Yo, Mom said to tell you we had room at the table." Joe smiled at me, then dropped his eyes to Teagan and stuck his hand out. "I'm Joe, Max's older brother. The better-looking one, and the one who regrets not finding you first."

Teagan giggled. Actually giggled, and Nico and I growled, which only made the asshole laugh.

The hostess walked up with menus prepared to seat us when to mine and Nico's shock, Joe waved her off. Then he grabbed Teagan's hand and placed it on his arm and started leading her to where the families sat at two large tables in the back. They were already shifting around to make room for us. Joe and Teagan reached the table first, and he started to pull a chair out for her.

"Stop, we are not sitting here," I said and the people who were chattering a mile a minute stopped and focused their eyes on me.

"Why not, Maximum? Are you embarrassed of

your family," my mother, Genieve, asked.

"Really, Mom? You are going with that as if this is some big coincidence," I said and looked down the table at Marianna and then back, "Generals in the army can't gather troops this quick."

"You're the one who mentioned where we were going," Nico said, and received a glare from my aunt, Angelina, who was his mother.

"You might as well join us, Max. Your uncle and I tried to squash this, and yet here we are," my dad said and spread his arms wide to encompass the entire group. I looked at Teagan and expected to see her scoping out the nearest exit. Instead, she was looking around the tables at our family members with a look of longing.

*Well damn.*

"Teagan," I said, and she turned and looked at Nico and I and smiled.

"What better way to learn about the two of you but from the people who know you best?" she asked and never gave us a chance to answer before she sat in the chair Joe had pulled out for her.

"That a girl! The adventurous type," Joe said and pushed her chair in and moved to his own. I looked at Nico, and he shrugged and took an empty seat beside Teagan.

"Fine," I said and took the empty chair on the other side of her.

"See, son, you're finally learning to go along with it," my dad said and smiled while Teagan laughed.

I met Nico's eyes over her head, and I figured we were thinking the same thing. We needed to make this a night to remember because after dinner with our families, we might never get another shot.

"I bet there was never a dull moment growing up," Teagan said. She had been going on about our families since we got into the truck. Her hands no longer timidly sat in her lap. One rested on my thigh as I drove, and she was holding hands with Nico with her other one.

"No. But then there was also never a quiet time either. Something was always going on," Nico told her.

"I would have loved that. Sometimes my house was too quiet with just my dad and me. The most company we ever had was holidays or on special occasions when my uncles joined us. To have such a large family, I envy you both."

Nico looked over at me when I glanced in his direction, his eyebrows raised. We'd both thought our families would have scared her off by the end of dinner, instead from the moment introductions were made, Teagan interacted with each of them as though she'd always been a part of the family. She laughed at the stories they told of Nico and me. And throughout the meal, she looked to have generally enjoyed herself.

From the looks we received from our mothers,

they totally approved. Teagan hadn't even seemed to mind the thousands of questions volleyed at her.

"So, you enjoyed yourself?" I asked as I maneuvered through the traffic.

"Are you kidding? Everyone was awesome. And I am looking forward to the shopping trip with your sisters and nieces." Teagan chuckled, then continued. "I can't believe you don't have one nephew. Max, how does Marianna manage with four girls? The whole family is beautiful. And Nico, oh my God, your sister, Cleo's, baby girl, with all that hair was absolutely adorable. Then, your sister, Sharee, announcing she was pregnant. To be included was so nice of them. I can't believe your brothers are not married. They are so sweet. And don't get me started on your moms and dads."

Nico and I wouldn't help but to laugh. Teagan looked between both of us, went quiet, and removed her hand from my thigh and pulled her other free from Nico's.

*Damn it.*

"Sorry, I hadn't thought until just now that umm...that I shouldn't have made plans with your sisters or agreed to let your mothers teach me how to cook some of their favorite recipes. I just got caught up and didn't think that you might not want me so involved in your family in case—"

"Stop!" I shouted as I pulled the SUV into a parking space in a lot designated for the beach on Pratt Boulevard.

"Don't yell at me. I was apologizing for my

actions with your families. My only excuse—"

"Did he not just tell you to stop?" Nico asked, interrupting her again. I turned the truck off, and Nico and I both turned toward her.

"Sorry for raising my voice and I'm sure Nico is, too." Nico agreed, and I continued. "But you pissed us off with the apology." I stopped when she frowned, and asked, "What?"

"You both laughed when I was talking about them, so I assumed." She shrugged.

"Well, there was your mistake. Assuming. We laughed, Teagan, because you were so excited about our families and it wasn't fake, it was genuine. We are around the craziness on a regular basis, so sometimes we forget how great they are. You reminded us of that with your enthusiasm from sharing dinner with them. We laughed because damn, we've known you for a few weeks and not once have we've even gotten a glimpse of this side of you. Plus, to talk about our family like you were... Teagan, they are too much for us sometimes, and you handled them as if you had always been a part of them," I stopped and look at Nico because I didn't know if I was getting across to her how it made me feel, so I was thankful when Nico jumped in.

"What he is trying to say, is we are glad you enjoyed our family and didn't run out the nearest exit. We like the fact you are comfortable around them. We might not know what this is," Nico waved hand between us, "but we want to find out.

Teagan, for us, it's a first."

Tears formed in her eyes but with all the women in our family, we learned quickly, the difference between sad and happy tears. I was glad I guessed right in this instance.

"I did enjoy your family, and I want to see where this leads," she whispered.

"Then let's get to the second part of the night," I said.

# Chapter Ten

## Teagan

I wiped a couple of tears away that had escaped my eyes and for the first time looked around where we sat parked.

"Oh, the Park Boulevard, I love walking to the end of the pier," I commented, and Nico opened the door and helped me out while Max got out on his side and went to the back of the SUV. He opened the hatch and when he stepped back, he held a blanket in one hand and a small cooler in the other.

On our way to the pier, Nico took the blanket from Max and draped it over his shoulder while Max carried the cooler. As we walked, Max reached for my hand with his free one and linked our fingers together. After of few more steps, Nico did the same, and the three of us walked hand in hand toward the pier.

"My dad and I would come out here sometimes and stand at the end and watch the water of Lake Michigan. It's calming. When I got older, my girlfriends and I started coming here, but they only came to scope out boys while I wanted to sit and enjoy the fresh air." I looked around as we walked up the stairs and onto the pier.

"Yeah, I bet the young boys were all over you. I would have done anything to get your attention," Max said and squeezed my hand, and I smiled up at him.

When we reached the end of the pier, Max let loose of my hand and draped his arm around my shoulder. I willingly moved into him; the warmth that radiated from his body felt nice against the cool breeze coming off the water. After a second, I felt his lips touch the top of my head.

Nico moved closer on my other side and let my hand go and placed his arm around my waist. We stood quietly and watched the ripple of the waves as the moon shined down on the water.

"Going to tell me what you have in the cooler?" I asked and looked up at Max.

"No, it's another little surprise."

"That's so not fair." I tried to pout but ended up unable to do it, and I chuckled at myself. Standing between the two men, their warmth wrapped around me, I couldn't imagine ever wanting to be anywhere else. I had even lost track of time to how long we stood there.

"Baby, you want to go sit on the beach?" Nico

110

asked, breaking the silence.

"I'd love that." And realized I really would. I'd been around them most of the day and evening, and I still wasn't ready for our time together to end.

"Then that is what we will do, sweetheart," Max said, and the three of us walked back toward the beach. A few people had had the same idea and sat on the beach watching the water. Other than that, there was very few people around. We walked further down, and I guessed for some privacy.

"If you get cold, baby, you let us know, okay?" Nico said.

"Okay. I'm fine right now. The wind is blowing, but at least it isn't too cold," I answered.

"After we pass the couple up ahead, we'll find a spot and unfold the blanket," Max said.

I saw the couple and for as far as I could see there wasn't anyone else on the beach so privacy would be plentiful if we went a little past them. As we drew closer to the couple, I noticed they were having a hard time placing their blanket down because of the wind. The guys must have noticed, too.

"Let's stop and help the couple, Nico," Max suggested.

"Sure," Nico said, and as we reached the couple, we stopped.

"Looks as if you could use a little help," Max said, sat the cooler down, then stepped up and grabbed a corner of the blanket just as the wind lifted it.

"Appreciate it. The wife and I have been fighting the damn thing for ten minutes," the man said. I took our blanket so Nico could help, too.

The men and the woman stretched the blanket out, then laid it down. While the men stood on their corners, the woman set a small cooler on her corner and gathered their shoes and placed them at the other corners.

"Not sure our shoes are going to hold the blanket down with this wind, Lauree," the man said to his wife. He turned and extended his hand out to shake first Max's, then Nico's. "I'm Bubba, and this is my wife, Lauree."

"Nice to meet you, I'm Max, this is Nico." Max pointed at Nico and then turned, grabbed my hand, and pulled me between them. "This is our girlfriend, Teagan."

I waited for the look of shock to appear on the couple's faces, but it never did. However, I thought I saw a small smile form on the woman's face before it quickly disappeared.

"They certainly picked the perfect nickname for Chicago. The windy city is right. We've been here since yesterday and I don't think it has stopped blowing once. Has it, babe?" the man looked at his wife and asked.

"No, it hasn't," Lauree answered, her voice soft as if she might be shy.

"So, you're not from around here?" I asked

Lauree. She shook her head.

"We're from Texas. Bubba surprised me with a weekend away," she answered, and her husband put his arm around her and pulled her into him.

"Ah, that is so sweet," I responded, and Lauree smiled, then looked at her husband but answered me.

"He can when he wants to be." The way she looked at him was how I imagined people deeply in love looked at one another. I looked at Max, and he was staring at me. When I turned my head the other way, Nico was doing the exact thing.

"We're headed home tomorrow, so I thought I would bring her to the beach for a little while to sit out under the stars and watch the water by moonlight. You folks made it a little more enjoyable by helping with the blanket," Bubba said.

"No problem. We're glad we could help you out," Nico said.

"Same here. We'll leave you to enjoy the moonlight with your wife. We plan to do the same with Teagan," Max exclaimed, and Nico and Bubba chuckled, picking up on Max's meaning while I'm sure my face was flushed because I suddenly felt heated. When I glanced at Lauree, her head was down, and I wasn't sure if she was blushing, too, or trying to hide the fact she was chuckling. Even with the moon out it was still too dark to make out.

We said goodbye to the couple and continued up the beach until we put a little distance between the couple and us to give us all a little privacy.

Once we our own blanket was spread out, we sat with me in the middle of the men and the cooler at our feet.

"Thank you for such a nice evening," I said and looked between the two.

"You're welcome, sweetheart," Max said and reached forward to open the cooler and pulled out three beers.

"You brought a cooler of beer as my surprise. Are you hoping to get me drunk?" I chuckled.

"Not just beer." Max leaned forward again after passing a beer to me and then to Nico.

"No wine?" I asked.

"Yeah, there's a bottle in there. Would you like wine instead, baby?" Nico asked, and I laughed. It seemed they thought of everything.

"I was just teasing. I'm not much of a wine drinker. I'm a beer kind of girl," I said and smiled at Nico.

"Good, because there's no wine in there." I shoved his shoulder and knew when he fell over it wasn't from my push.

"Asshole," I said and laughed, so he would know I was teasing.

"Soon," Nico said as he sat back up. And it took a minute for what he said to register.

"Oh my God, you did not just say that!" Nico looked at me, and with the moon glowing, I was able to make out the smirk on his face.

"Not if it isn't something you like or want to try. Hell yes if you do. But no pressure, baby," he said and nudged me with his shoulder.

I noticed Max pulled out a covered container and sat holding it as he watched us. I couldn't decipher the look on his face. Both men seemed to be waiting for me to answer.

"I've never tried it before. I wanted to and when I brought it up to the last guy I was seeing, he...well we never got around to it." I reached for the container and Max held it over his head.

"I'll hand this to you after you tell us what the guy said, sweetheart." I stared at Max but didn't answer. When Nico's breath hit my ear, a shiver ran through me.

"Answer Max, baby. You can tell us anything," Nico whispered in my ear as one of his hands caressed my neck.

"He said it was nasty and if I liked those types of things, then maybe he wasn't the man for me," I admitted in a low voice.

"Damn fuckin' straight he wasn't the man for you. No real man would deny his woman anything he was capable of giving," Max said and handed me the container like he promised if I told them.

I never thought of myself as a woman who needed a man to protect and take care her but then again, other than my dad and uncles, I never had one show much interest in wanting to. More or less two, that showed Max's and Nico's fierceness and loyalty.

"What did you do when he said that? And, Teagan, if you cried, you are giving us the dumbshit's name because he needs to be schooled!" I burst out laughing at the look of absolute menace on Nico's face.

I pulled myself together, then confessed, "I told him that he would never have to worry about me asking for something like that again." I didn't get to finish before Nico and Max cursed, and by the veins protruding at their temples, I rushed to get the rest out, "Wait, let me finish." They both stared at me, waiting or maybe they were unable to speak, I wasn't sure which one. "He said 'good' in response, and I got off the couch, grabbed my purse, and headed toward the door. When he asked where I was going, I told him to find a real man who liked real women, then I suggested he needed to loosen up, and he could start by fucking himself."

Both men blinked, and as fast as their tempers flared, they deflated, and they both started laughing.

"Open that container and feed us some brownies, sweetheart." Max leaned back on his elbows.

"Hey, how is feeding you two brownies my surprise?" I queried.

"Cause you want to take care of your men," Nico said and chuckled.

"Pfft, my men. You haven't even kissed me." Caught up in the teasing, it was out of my mouth before I thought about what I was saying. Once I had, I was getting ready to apologize when the

116

container was ripped out of my hands, and I found myself flat on my back with Max leaning over me, his face inches from mine.

"So, there's no doubt in your head," was all he said before his mouth took mine. And took was exactly what he did.

Max asked for no permission to enter as he pushed his tongue in and tasted every crevice of my mouth. He rested most of his weight on his elbows, and his hands ran through the sides of my hair until he had strands wrapped around them. He tilted my head to get a better angle, and I felt my body relax. The kiss heated, and so did my core. So much so, I rubbed my thighs together to find some relief.

When Max pulled away, we were both breathing heavily. My breath started to level when Nico's face came into view.

"We're yours. Never doubt it," Nico said before his lips met mine. Nico was more gentle but no less lethal. His tongue ran across my lips, and he bit down on the bottom and then sucked. The next pass of his tongue, he pressed it against my lips, and when I parted mine, he slipped easily in, tasting everywhere his tongue reached. My body started to react. If possible, I would have melted into the sand. He rested his weight on his elbows like Max had done, but instead of latching onto my hair, his hands rested against the sides of my face while his thumbs caressed my cheeks. He took what he needed and gave me what I wanted in a

117

kiss that should have been classified as sweet but instead the pace was steady and left me wanting it to never end.

Nico broke the kiss and sat up. I stayed laid out on the blanket and closed my eyes. Minutes had to have passed before Max's voice broke through the haze and I opened my eyes.

"Now that you've been kissed. How about those brownies?" he asked.

"You're an asshole," I said and shook my head, then sat up.

"Doesn't change the fact we left no doubt, does it?" I looked between the two and then grabbed the container.

"Wasn't I supposed to be feeding my men brownies?" I said sarcastically.

"Damn straight," they both said in unison.

I fed them brownies, and they fed some to me. We drank beer, we talked, and we laughed. The longer we sat there, it hit me I was experiencing what the phrase 'falling in love' was meant for. And it was accurate because I was pretty sure I was.

When we got ready to leave, they asked me to come to their house, and it seemed the most natural thing to say yes.

No thinking, no hesitation. Just yes.

# Chapter Eleven

## Teagan

In the back of my mind, I knew what would happen when I agreed to the date. So going to their home after we'd had the best evening together wasn't a hard decision. All the time we'd spent together at the gym had been leading up to it. Getting to know them, and their families, made it all the easier to accept them both. Max's and Nico's personalities complimented each other. Both had a sweet and caring side, but Nico was calm, where Max was high-strung. Their similarities were many, from looks, loyalty to family and friends, and how they knew who they were and accepted it. Not afraid to go after what they wanted.

We pulled up to the house and waited for the garage door to open, and I took the opportunity and stared out the window at their home. Even in

119

the dark, the front was illuminated by lighting, which looked as if it had been strategically placed to showcase it. The house to the landscape around it was beautifully done, too. After Max pulled into the garage and parked the car, we got out and entered the house through the kitchen. It was open and large, and the granite counters and the stainless-steel appliances blended well with the cabinetry and flooring.

"Want a tour?" Max asked.

"Most definitely. If the rest is like what I have seen so far, I bet it is beautiful."

"Come on, we'll take you on the grand tour," Nico said and grabbed ahold of my hand.

The brownstone was old, but the care taken in restoring it to its original appearance showed in every room we went through. The time and patience that had been put into the home reflected on its owners.

"Do family members stay with you often? This place is huge," I said as we walked out of Nico's bedroom after I'd viewed Max's.

"No, everyone lives around here. Though occasionally one of the nieces will stay over," Max said as we headed to the end of the hall to the last door on the second floor. Nico pushed it open and flipped the switch on the wall that turned on a lamp on the nightstand. I walked into the room in awe. It held the biggest bed I'd ever seen, and the accents in the room were in neutral shades. The room was large enough for the bed set, and even included a small sitting area off to one side. There were two other doors in the room: one to a large walk-in closet, and the other into the master bath. The bathroom alone was the size of a small bedroom with a sunken jet tub, dual sinks, its own linen closet, and an oversized walk-in glass fronted shower.

"Why didn't one of you take this room? You could have flipped for it or something," I said as I stepped back into the bedroom. When I didn't receive a response, I turned to look at the guys. They had stopped just outside the bathroom door. Each stared at me, their faces held a look that had me worried I'd overstepped. "Sorry, none of my business." I started toward the doorway, which led into hallway.

"Teagan," Max called out and I stopped.

"It's okay. I shouldn't have asked," I answered, feeling ackward. I didn't turn around because I felt the heat rise on my face from embarrassment. With one question that really wasn't any of my business, I put a damper on an awesome evening.

When I didn't receive, yet another response, I started toward the door again. Before I was able to make my escape, arms wrapped around me from behind, and lips touched the skin where my neck and shoulder met. I stood frozen as the lips kissed up my neck until they stopped by my ear.

"We fixed this room for when we found the special woman to share our life with," Nico whispered, then he began to kiss his way back down my neck. I found myself tilting my head to give him better access. A shiver ran through my body when he moved his hands to rub up and down my arms. I closed my eyes, which caused the feelings to intensify.

My eyes snapped back open when Max press against my front. One of his hands grabbed my hip while the other caressed my face until his fingers weaved into my hair. He wrapped my hair around his hand and pulled until my face was upturned and I was looking directly into his eyes.

"Be that woman for us," was all Max said before his mouth met mine. The kiss was far from gentle as he devoured me. His tongue pressed against my lips, and I opened, giving him what he wanted. He explored every inch of my mouth with his tongue. I moaned. At least I thought it was me, but I wasn't sure.

Nico's lips were making a trail across my shoulder, and he used mouth to push my shirt off my shoulder, followed by the thin bra strap, baring more of my skin to him. He moved one of his hands to the opposite hip while Max continued to have a hold on the other. Nico slipped his hand between Max and me, and his fingers slid under the hem of my shirt. Then he splayed his hand on my stomach and pulled me against him. Close enough I felt his hardened cock as it pressed into me.

The sensations that coursed through my body from their touches left no doubt for me that I would do anything for the two of them. What did that say about me? I'd dated men. I'd slept with them to take care of my needs when I wanted more than what I gave myself. But not once when I accepted the pleasure the others had given me had I felt an effect with such magnitude. Max and Nico together were explosive.

How was it possible to feel as though I'd known the two of them a lifetime?

Max released my hair and my lips. His hand moved to the side of my neck and slide down my shoulder and arm. In no time his hand was at my waist, and he grabbed the bottom of my shirt and lifted it. He stepped away just enough and with the help from Nico, my shirt was up and over my head and tossed to the floor in record time.

Nico's hands slipped around to the front, and in one twist of his fingers, the clasp on my bra gave way. My breasts heavy with need spilled out, and Max's hands were there to capture them. As he squeezed and kneaded my breasts, Nico removed my bra, and it joined my shirt on the floor.

Max bent and placed his mouth over one of my peaked nipples, his tongue circling, rolling it against the roof of his mouth as he sucked and continued to caress the other breast.

I'd lost all track of my surroundings as my head dropped back. I hadn't even realized what Nico had been up to until my jeans and panties were pooled at my feet.

"Lift your foot, baby," I followed Nico's soft-spoken words by lifting first one foot and then the other. He slipped my shoes and socks off as he removed the other garments.

My realization as to the effect their touches brought was when I bumped into the bed. Somehow, they had moved us across the room, and it hadn't even registered with me.

Max released my breasts from his hand and mouth to push me back onto the bed, my legs dangling in front since my feet couldn't reach the floor. When I gained enough of myself to notice what was happening around me, I saw Max and Nico in their naked glory. And yes, it was glory. I've seen them shirtless plenty of times but never completely bare. Their cocks were hard, big, and thick, and as I watched, the veins pulsed in rhythm with their heartbeats. I felt a surge of moisture between my legs and the need to rub them together to bring the relief my body required.

"Well damn, baby. That is a surprise," at Max's words, Nico looked at him and then followed the direction of where Max's eyes were focused. I knew what they saw. When I first started as a trainer at the gym, I had a small set of boxing gloves tattooed on my right hipbone.

"Ah, sweetheart, that is hot as hell. How long have you had that?" I didn't know if I could answer Nico because Max moved, bent my legs, and planted my feet flat on the bed. His hands rubbed from my knees to my thighs. He spread me wide and lowered until his mouth touched center. His tongue moved through my folds from back to front,

124

and when he sucked my clit into his mouth, I closed my eyes and let him take over my body until the only thing surrounding me was he and Nico. Max pulled back, and I wanted to cry out.

"Did you forget how to talk, sweetheart?" Max smirked.

I arched and screamed in frustration, "Please don't stop!"

Max's mouth returned, and his tongue flicked my clit, then pushed into me, mimicking what I couldn't wait for him to do with his cock. I knew they were waiting for me to answer but how was that possible when my breath was nonexistent?

The bed dipped from Nico's weight as he moved to lay on the bed beside me. He placed his lips on my neck and then began a path down, his teeth nipping until his mouth settled on my breast. He laved, suckled, and bit at the same time Max's tongue speared my core. The orgasm ripped through me, and my scream echoed in the room.

I came down from my orgasm only to realize they'd switched places. Max was stretched out beside me, his hands caressing me. A palm laid flat on my stomach and his one hand big enough to span from hipbone to hipbone. These men made me feel dainty as they surrounded me.

Max's lips touched mine. His hardness to my softness, I bit his lip, and he opened, letting me explore his mouth. His taste mixed with my own as I held him to me by his hair.

Nico had taken Max's place between my legs.

He lifted them over his shoulders, putting me on full display. I should have been embarrassed or maybe felt some type of shame for being with two men, but none came. Only moans sounded as Nico's finger breached my pussy while he tongued my clit, and his thumb circled my back hole.

Max pulled away, and I heard the drawer to the nightstand open.

"You're going to need to lube her up good, Nico. She needs to be stretched. We don't want to ruin her first experience by hurting her."

Nico let go of my clit and pulled his finger out. The next thing I felt was a cool wetness as it ran from my pussy to my butthole. Nico's fingers spread the lube, then he pushed a finger back into my pussy and moved it in circles, spreading the lube and coating my entrance, stretching me to make their way easier.

When he touched my back hole and pushed his thumb past the rim, my hips jerked. The sting was minimal to the feeling of pleasure that started to take over as he began to pump in and out while Max caressed my breasts and played with my nipples.

"Easy, baby, we will get you there. Need to make our path a little easier to slip into." When he finished talking, he removed his thumb, only to be replaced with first one figure before he added another.

My heated body shivered from the coolness of the lube, and I squeezed my eyes closed and let

Nico's and Max's movements bring me to the edge of orgasm. Just as it was in reach, Max moved away, and the loss of him and the orgasm I so desperately needed.

I opened my eyes when Max's cock pushed against my lips demanding entrance. I grabbed the base only to find I was unable to wrap my hand completely around his girth. I ran my thumb over the tip and gathered the pre-cum, using it to make the slide of my hand easier as I pumped him a few times before I opened my mouth and took him in. His salty taste exploded on my tongue as my actions brought more pre-cum dripping from the tip. His groans reflected the pleasure I was bringing him.

"Goddamn, take more of me, sweetheart. Your mouth is fucking heaven. As soon as Nico has you stretched, you are going to be ours. There will be no turning back. The three of us are going to see where this leads us."

I sucked him deep until Max's cock hit the back of my throat, then I hummed, and the vibrations stopped him from saying anything else.

"You ready for the ride of your life, baby. No need to answer. I know you are enjoying Max's cock. Your cream coating my fingers and hand gave it away. If we'd known that sucking his dick was going to have your juices flowing, we could have bypassed the lube."

Max pulled his cock out of my mouth and laid back. He pulled me up and over him until I

127

straddled his hips, the head of his cock poised at my entrance. Nico's efforts paid off when Max thrust up and pulled me down at the same time, filling me. The head of his cock touched against my cervix until our pubic bones touched, and the orgasm I had lost was back and pulsed through me. I clenched around Max as my body shook.

"Shit, I'm going to blow before we even get started," Max said as I looked into his dark brown eyes and saw desire for me. How was it even possible to fall so quickly for two men? But I was, and at the moment I didn't care. I refused to ruin whatever was beginning between us by overthinking any there was no way to explain it, and at the moment, I didn't care.

Max pulled out, and Nico kissed my shoulder, then pushed me forward until Max and I were chest to chest. I felt pressure against my rim right before he breached it. Nico paused, rubbed my back, then worked his way deeper into me. He slowly moved in and out until he was fully seated.

I lifted my face, wanting Max's mouth. He placed a hand on each side of my head. The kiss was soft, then demanding. I wasn't sure how much more my system to take.

Nico pulled out and Max broke our kiss. Nico's hands lifted my hips, while Max slid his hand between us and position his cock at my entrance again. Nico pushed me down on Max's cock. He then worked his cock back into my back hole and set the pace.

My breath came as pants as Nico moved faster. His efforts taking all three of us to the point of no return. The pressure built within me, Nico hitting a spot inside me I didn't know existed. The dual sensations were bringing me to my breaking point.

Nico bottomed out with one last thrust, and the warmth of his release had me clawing at Max's chest and rolling the hoops in his nipples as I tried to reach for the orgasm to take me over the edge with him.

"Come on, sweetheart, take me with you," Max gritted out, and I raised up and down on him until my walls squeezed around his cock. I felt it twitch inside me, then he filled me with his cum as tremors racked my body.

After we cleaned up, we settled back onto the bed, and I snuggled between the two men. Like all little girls, I dreamt of the perfect man. The one meant to be mine forever.

I closed my eyes and let the little girl dream turn into a grown woman's reality. How lucky was I to have two men?

# Chapter Twelve

## Max

"Fuck, it can't be morning already," Nico said and rolled over, taking Teagan with him.

"It's someone's freakin' phone." I got out of the bed and followed the sound until I stood over Teagan's jeans. I bent down and grabbed them to search the pockets as the ringing continued. I pulled it out and fumbled it, catching it before it hit the ground.

"Can you find that fucker and shut it off?" Nico mumbled.

"Shut up, dick. I'm trying."

"Well, you two are pleasant in the morning," Teagan said, and I looked over at the bed and she hadn't even opened her eyes.

"It's not morning, baby. It's still dark outside," Nico said as he cracked one eye and looked toward the window.

131

The ringing had stopped by the time I had caught the cell before it hit the floor. As I lifted it closer to my face, a beep sounded indicating a voicemail message.

"Oh, then carry on. But can you do it quietly, I'm trying to sleep." I shook my head as I watched her shove her head under my pillow.

"Sweetheart, it was your phone. You have a message." I sat on the side of the bed and waited for her to sit up. She moved the pillow and rolled to her side and held her hand out. I gave her the phone, and she hit some buttons.

"It's my dad. He wouldn't have called if it wasn't important," she said and sat up in bed with the phone against her ear.

The mention of Teagan's dad had Nico sitting up in bed.

"He asked me to call him as soon as I got the message." She started punching buttons and waited for someone to answer. "Dad, what's going on? Is everything okay?" she fired off as soon as her dad answered, then went quiet.

Nico and I both were up and gathering our clothes off the floor while we waited to hear what was going on.

"Okay, I'll be there in about fifteen minutes." Teagan hit the end button and jumped out of bed. "I have to go to the gym. Dad wouldn't say much other than the police were there because he caught someone breaking and entering." She started yanking on her clothes and Nico and I did the same.

"Ready?" I asked as she looked in the mirror and tried to comb her hair with her fingers.

"Yeah, a shower would have been nice but no time." She looked at Nico, then at me, and back to the mirror at herself. "This should be interesting. Nothing like showing up at a B&E with cops present, looking like you have been well fucked." She slipped her feet into her shoes.

"Would you rather look badly fucked?" I asked as we headed out of the room.

"Asshole," she said as we walked downstairs.

"If there wasn't time for a shower, I don't think there is time for that either," Nico said as we entered the garage.

"Can't you be serious for a minute," Teagan said as Nico helped her into the truck.

"Sweetheart, we're trying to lighten the mood. Nothing we can do until we get there and find out what happened."

"I know. I can't believe someone tried to break in the gym. Anything worth money is too heavy to just walk out with," she surmised.

"Won't take us long to get there." I back out of the garage, hit the button to close the door and backed out onto the street. Once we were on our way, I pushed down on the gas and prayed no cops laid in wait. I knew Teagan wasn't just thinking about the break-in, she was more than likely worried about her dad.

When we turned down the block where the

gym was located, I saw two police cars out front. There was no ambulance or EMTs from the fire department, which I would take as a good sign. I pulled up in front and parked.

Nico had barely gotten out the passenger door when Teagan was out and on her way around him. If Nico had been any slower, our girl would have mowed his ass over.

We walked in, and Teagan stopped. "Milton?! What the fuck?"

Before Nico or I could ask who Milton was, I noticed Kearney and one of the police officers headed toward us. The other officer stood off to the side with a man, who looked to be in his thirties, dressed in black pants, black shirt, and camo paint on his face. I guessed that had to be Milton.

Teagan didn't wait for her dad to reach us before she started in, "Did he say why the hell he was trying to break into the gym? Damn idiot should be glad I wasn't here."

"Teagan, if you hold on, I'll tell you what happened," Kearney answered.

"Fine, start from the beginning. Because every scenario that ran through my mind on the way here, the ending didn't have Milton in handcuffs." Teagan looked at the man and glared. "Depending on what my dad says, will depend on if I give a crap the cops are here, and kick your ass anyway." Teagan pointed at the man, and I swear I saw the officer's, who was beside Milton, lips twitch.

134

"I couldn't sleep, and you know when that happens, I come down and hit on one of the bags for a little while." At Teagan's nod, Kearney continued. "I came out of the backroom strapping on my gloves, and I saw a shadow lurking by the window, so I ducked into the office and called the police. I waited in the dark behind the wall in the hallway and watched. He tried to pick the lock but wasn't having any luck with it, so he kicked it until the frame gave way.

"When it did, he walked in and pushed the door closed. Guess he thought if the cops drove by, they wouldn't be able to tell. He turned on a flashlight and started walking in my direction. I was going to duck into the locker room until I saw it was Milton. I hit the switches on the wall and lit the whole damn place up. I thought the jackass was going to piss his pants.

"I walked out of the back and asked him what the hell did he think he was doing, and the little prick lunged at me at the same time the two cop cars pulled up. I landed an uppercut to his chin and Milton was on the floor, out cold when the cops walked in." Kearney shrugged.

"Teagan, who is the douche?" I asked because the guy looked too soft to have ever spent time in a gym, either as an employee or someone who worked out.

"I went out with him a few times. I broke it off," she said but didn't look at Nico and me.

"Because he was a pansy ass," Kearney

commented, and I snorted.

"Dad, can we not get into why you don't like Milton and more into why he decided to break in here?" Teagan stressed.

"They are arresting him for breaking and entering along with the intent of some sort. When he came to, they cuffed him and then searched inside and outside. They found a gas can on the side of the building," Kearney said, disgustedly and glanced in Milton's direction.

"How do you know it was his? I mean, you didn't catch him with it," Nico asked the officer beside Kearney.

"No, we didn't. But his car is parked up the street with two more filled gas cans in the trunk," the officer answered.

"He also had matches and a couple old rags shoved in his pockets," Kearney added and shook his head.

"Did you get a reason out of him?" I asked and looked over at Milton, who was staring at Teagan.

"No. He clammed up after giving us his name, which Mr. O'Hagan had already given to us," the officer answered.

"How many times did you hit him, Dad?" Teagan sounded tired, it was going on four in the morning, and we'd only been asleep a couple hours when the call came.

"Sir, we're taking Mr. Hawthorn in. If you have any more questions or remember anything else, call the number listed on this," the officer interrupted and handed Kearney a card before he had a chance to answer Teagan.

"I hope his ass gets nailed to the wall by the judge, and by his cellmate," Kearney said as he took the card.

"Dad!" Teagan scolded while Nico and I chuckled. The officer snorted, then went to help the other officer with Milton.

"So, got a KO, and saved the gym," I boasted and smiled when Kearney looked at me.

"Did I disturb you three when I called?" He looked each of us over, and that's when I remembered what we looked like—wrinkled clothes and all.

"Stop it, Dad. I'm a grown woman, and it's not like I haven't had sex. Hell, you took me to the clinic to get on birth control." The words were no sooner out of her mouth, and it hit me. Nico's under the breath "shit", confirmed he realized, too, that neither of us remembered condoms. We'd been in such a rush to take her; we had pounced without a thought. Thank God for the birth control pills because with everything going on, we didn't need a baby. At least not right now.

Teagan had to have sensed what was going through our minds because she looked at us and rolled her eyes.

As the officers began to lead Milton to the door, he glared at Teagan and sneered, "Guess you found what you were looking for. You could have at least gone a step above a gym ra—"

I stepped forward, and before I could say or do anything, Milton's head snapped back. Teagan grabbed her hand while the officer pulled Milton toward the door. As they were going through the door, one of the officers said, "I would think after you got your ass knocked out that you would learn to keep your mouth shut. Both Father and daughter in one day."

I grabbed Teagan's arm, so not to touch the hand and held it up for Nico and me to look at.

"That's going to bruise and hurt, sweetheart." I laid a kiss on her knuckles.

"Let's get some ice on it, baby, and then you can lay down," Nico said, and I agreed. We could all use a few more hours of sleep.

"No one is going to sleep. We have five weeks to train for the first round of bouts. You two need to be ready. I can ice my hand. Daly will be here in a couple hours. Go home, get a shower, something to eat, and then get back here. We have work to do."

"We have workout clothes here, and we can use the showers in the locker room. Then we can fix the front door before we grab something to eat. You need to eat, too. By the time all of that is done, Daly should be here, and we can start our workout," I brought up.

"Fine. Come upstairs when you're done, and I'll fix you some breakfast." Teagan turned and headed toward the back. After she was out of sight, Kearney faced us.

138

"She's going to be tougher on herself than on the three of you. I won't be able to go to the away bouts. Someone needs to be at the gym. I'm going to need you two to watch out for her."

"You got it," Nico and I both said.

"You have a long road ahead. I guarantee if you make it there, every drop of sweat will have been worth it." Kearney patted us on our backs and started toward the back with Nico and I on his heels.

It promised to be one long ass day and a longer five weeks. In the end, we'd get to wake up and start it all over again. Our lives together and in the ring would be clocked by six-week intervals. The goal for each of us when it was all said and done would be to have the experience to last a lifetime.

# Chapter Thirteen

## Teagan

*Boston...*

TD Garden. We arrived two days ago to allow the guys ample time to get into a routine and work through the anxiousness. I knew the bouts weren't only for Daly, Nico, and Max. They were for me, too.

Can a woman trainer/manager bring a winner into the ring or octagon?

I wasn't only bringing one—I brought three.

The last five weeks had been long in some ways and shorter in others. Weeks of preparation for fifteen minutes or if you counted the breaks the total amount of time in the ring was eighteen minutes.

Daly, Nico, and Max worked out six days a

week without complaint. At least regarding their workouts. Max and Nico hadn't cared too much when I dropped the no sex rule one week out from bouts. They tried every way imaginable to get me to break that rule, but I stayed steady.

As we got out of the rental, I ran through the list in my head to make sure we had everything needed. I watched the three men hoist the shoulder straps of their bags, lifting them out of the trunk. Max slammed the trunk closed, and we made our journey across the parking lot.

"I asked your dad if he would pack your stuff and we could get our brothers to pick it up and take it to the house," Max said and casually placed his arm over my shoulder as we walked toward the entrance.

"I can pack my own things. The two of you are going to make me crazy," I said and sighed.

"Glad I wasn't included in that," Daly said, then chuckled and walked ahead of us.  Nico and Max flipped him off.

"You are dragging your feet, baby," Nico said and nudged my shoulder.

"I am not. I already stay most of the time at your house, so how is that dragging my feet," I argued.

"Every other night. Sweetheart, you told your dad you were a grown woman. Can I point out that he is a grown man?" Max brought up. In the last three weeks, after they'd asked me to officially move in, Nico and he had each referenced my dad

142

and I being grown people who were able to make up their own minds.

The 'I love yous' hadn't been said but they showed it in other ways. I wasn't going to complain because I hadn't said it to them. I'd fallen quickly from our first date at the beach. Was it possible I was holding out for the words? Maybe.

"No, you're not allowed to point that out to me. I know I am having trouble leaving my dad by himself. I'm working on it. Why are we discussing this when you should be concentrating on your upcoming fights?" I stressed. I had no desire to get into another discussion on my unwillingness to leave my dad alone. I knew the reason was because it had been him and me for years. My dad had given up his dream to raise me while morning the loss of his wife. It felt as though I was abandoning him, which was totally crazy because I would see the man every day at the gym.

"We'll win the bouts. Stop stressing over it," Nico emphasized.

"However, your dad can't seem to gain his freedom," Max said, and I stopped walking and looked at him.

"My dad wants to be free of me?" I muttered.

"Damn, Max," Nico grumbled and shook his head, which only made me more curious as to what Max meant.

"I'm not taking another step until you tell me what you mean by that, Max," I stressed and crossed my arms.

"Dumbass!" Shawn yelled over his shoulder as he continued to walk toward the entrance.

Max squeezed my shoulder and looked down at me. Indecision was apparent on his face. I was so pleased with my dad's easy acceptance of Max and Nico. The bond seemed to be growing daily between the three of them.

Now, not so much.

"Fine. But first let me say that you call us assholes when we demand answers," Max huffed.

"Dig your own hole. Don't pull my ass under the bus with you. I haven't been laid in a goddamn week, and I have had a warm woman in bed beside me. So yeah, I'm getting a little testy. I'm going to win my bout because I'm sure my dick, which has been hard the whole time I've went without, could be a new move against my opponent. Win by dick stab!" Nico said loudly.

"You're bringing no sex before a bout up in the parking lot. Your discomfort has nothing to do with why my dad wants free of me!" I yelled back. I was being irrational, but I didn't quite give a shit.

"Actually, it sort of does," Max answered, and I looked up at him.

"Nico's issue with no sex the week before a fight has to do with my dad. So help me if you complained to him about the no sex thing, I'm going to kick both your asses," I threatened, knowing it was an empty one. No way I would be able to take either one of them unless I fought dirty. "I love that you are getting close to my dad,

144

but talking sex with him, is creepy."

"We are not talking about our sex lives with your dad, baby. Give us some credit. We should move this conversation inside, that black car has circled us three times. Our luck they'll call the damn cops, thinking we are fighting," Nico groused and looked around the lot.

"No, I want to know right now what is going on with my dad," I snapped and frowned at them.

"For fuck's sake, sweetheart, he is seeing a woman. Maybe he would like to bring her back to his house. You know, run around naked or bend her over the ropes," Max revealed.

I barely heard the ropes comment because I placed my hands over my ears.

"Baby, he raised you," Nico said as he pulled my hands from my ears and looked me in the eyes. "The man loves you more than anything in this world. You and he will always have a special bond. But with you spending a lot of time with us, he's lonely, honey."

I'd been so wrapped up in the guys training for the upcoming fights that I hadn't looked closely at my dad. If there were ever a man who deserved his own happiness it was my dad. He'd given up a lot for me.

"I'm the crappiest daughter," I responded and raised my hand to stop Nico and Max from arguing with me. "Call your brothers. I would appreciate any help moving my stuff into your house."

"Sweetheart, you're not a crappy daughter.

You've just had a lot on your mind," Max said and dropped his arm from my shoulder to run his hand down my back.

"Yet you figured it out, Maximum Masetti!" I yelled.

The black car Nico mentioned earlier pulled up beside us and the window lowered as it stopped.

"Is there something wrong or a problem? Maybe something I could help you with?" Came from the brunette behind the wheel, who looked Max and Nico over as she spoke. It wasn't hard to imagine what she would like to help them with— her and her DD size breasts.

"Run along with your melons back to skanksrus," I blurted.

Max grabbed one arm and Nico the other and they started moving us closer to the entrance.

"Going to put this out there, baby. I think you are suffering more from the no sex rule than us," Nico said, and before I could reply, Shawn pushed open the entrance door.

"I was coming to get you. The time changed on my bout and Nico's. Max's is the only one that stayed the same."

"They do that sometimes. It is to draw more people in early, hoping they will stay through all the fights. More money to the center's concession. What time are you up?" I asked as I stepped inside.

"One hour," Shawn answered.

"Shit, let's get a move on it," I said, and walked through the door. Showtime was sixty minutes away.

We made it ringside with two minutes to spare. I knew the change in times was the commission screwing around with my guys. The committee were split down the middle on having a woman trainer/manager as publicity and the other half not wanting a woman intruding into the sacred boys' club.

After Shawn had notified us of the time changes, we ran in, found our locker room, which was at the end of the dang hallway that stretched the entire length of the building. By the time Shawn was ready, and we made it to the ring, the stats of the fighters were being announced.

The round started and Shawn hadn't had his mind on it. His opponent owned him in the round. Luckily, it had been the last one he had swept. The fighter's trainer would be chewing his ass for trying to make the bout last longer. I taught my guys to always take an opportunity when it's there. Shawn's opponent had had two open shots and he skirted them. His mistake would be Shawn's break.

"You got this, Shawn. You've done the time preparing. Look at him. He didn't have to work out six days a week for five weeks straight to be here. Now show him you want it more!"

Shawn nodded and moved to the center of the ring. No one in the place had seen it coming, including me. It seemed my guys had been doing a little secret practicing on their own.

The second round started and Shawn charged, wrapped his opponent up, and dumped him to the mat. Shawn had followed him down and pinned the guy's arms to his sides with his knees. The forearm to the throat was a Max move all the way. Welterweights have more finesse because the men have more agility at the lighter weight. Most lacked the power to put enough pressure to make the other fighter tap out.

Max sat behind us in one of the extra chairs, and when Shawn got his opponent down, he yelled for the final move.

"Put your shoulder strength into it and keep your hips in place or he will roll you!" Max yelled, and I grinned. The guys had definitely been having extra workouts without me around.

The crowd yelled when the referee bent over to watch the move closely. With the fighter's arms pinned and due to Shawn's legs being in the way, it was hard to see his hands. The referee spoke to the fighter, and before I comprehended what had happened, Shawn was on his feet with his arm held up. The fight belonged to him. One fight closer to the belt.

Only one bout was between the welterweight and the light heavyweight, but it was enough time for me to get Nico ready. The walk to the ring the second time was a little easier with one win down.

"What was Shawn's time again?" Nico asked while we waited for the referee to signal the fighters to center ring.

"Five minutes nine seconds, why?" I answered as Nico bounced on his toes in front of me.

"I needed to know what to shoot for," he said, then stepped toward the middle of the ring for the beginning of the fight.

It took Nico a couple of minutes to settle down, but when he did, his opponent was helpless to stop the punishment. Nico was relentless.

If the rest of the fighters who stood in the way of my guys becoming World Champions in their weight classes, then the titles were as good as theirs already.

The bell signaled round one was over and when Nico sat in the chair, he hadn't even been breathing hard from the exertion.

"He's yours, Nico. The only thing he has going for him is fast feet. Corner him, and you'll own him," I instructed.

Nico nodded and tipped the water bottle up and drank. Max and Shawn both yelled at Nico, showing their support. Max's fight would be the last of the night, it would be hard on him to wait, but I hoped when the fight ended, all the waiting would be worth it.

The bell rang, round two started and Nico did exactly what I told him. He got his opponent in the corner, and with jabs to the abdomen had the fighter doubling over. The knee Nico brought up and into the fighter's face sprayed blood on the spectators in the front row seat. Nico followed the move with an uppercut, and it was his opponent's downward fall. Nico stepped back and to the side, and the fighter fell forward to the mat.

The crowd chanted for Nico as the final decision was read and he was acknowledged as the winner.

Something passed between Nico and Max as Max congratulated him. With two fights down, it was hard not thinking ahead to New York. However with this sport, I learned never to look ahead. Focus needed to stay on the fighter directly in front of you. Looking past an opponent gave them an advantage. Sometimes a very lethal one.

I entered the locker room and turned, and noticed Nico was the only one who came in the room behind me. I looked at him, prepared to ask where Max and Shawn were when the raw desire in Nico's eyes lodged the words in my throat and buckled my knees. He stalked toward me as if I was his prey. The power of each step he took toward me was exhilarating and terrifying at the same time.

Nico reached me, grabbed my shoulders, and turned me around to face the table in the room. His arms surrounded me and the nose in the crook of my neck slid up and down. The bite was unexpected but had my head tilting to the side. He pulled me back against him, and I felt his cock at my backside: long, hot, and hard. When he pushed his hips into me, I felt myself grow damp, and my stomach clenched from desire.

150

Nico's hands worked their way under my shirt, and he squeezed my breasts. He pinched my nipples through the thin material of my bra, and my core spasmed as if protesting its emptiness.

I found myself pushing back against him. I wiggled my hips trying to get closer, wanting him to take me.

"Does my baby need it as bad as I do?" Nico asked, pulled the front of my bra down and twisted my peaked nipples, and I moaned. He removed his hands from under my shirt, and I wanted to protest, but the words were stuck in my throat as he shoved on my back, bending me over the table.

In no time, my pants, panties, and shoes were yanked down and off.

Nico used his knees to spread my legs wider, then he stepped into me and his cock slid through my folds, coating it with my juices.

"You are so wet and ready for me, baby. Stretch your arms out and grab hold of the table's edge." I did what he asked and was rewarded with the head of his cock poised at my entrance. "Hold on tight," was whispered in my ear as he leaned his body over mine.

The wait wasn't long, and he entered me with one hard thrust. I gasped, pushed back against him, and moaned as I buried my face on the top of the table. Nico pulled out, the head of his cock at my entrance. He lifted off me only to place his large hands on my ass, he splayed them, and used his thumbs to spread my cheeks open, then he shoved back into the hilt.

"I like watching you take my cock, baby. Your pussy is greedy to be filled." As he talked, he repeated the motion, pulling out and then slamming back in.

Every time he slammed back in, his heavy balls slapped against my clit, the motion had my orgasm forming quickly. When he picked up speed, I knew he was almost there, too.

Nico thrust into me one last time, and we crested together. His weight slumped against me as my head laid on the table and we worked to catch our breaths.

"If it's going to be like this every time after a fight, I think I can deal with the no sex before rule," he whispered in my ear.

"Me, too," I muttered, and felt his chest vibrate against me as he chuckled.

# Chapter Fourteen

## Max

As I stood in the middle of the ring and faced my opponent, I knew this was what all the hours of training were for. My opponent and I were the last fight of the night. I was in the zone, and there was nothing to stop me from being the victor.

In fifteen minutes of play, I would move forward while the fighter in front of me called it a day. The sport was brutal, but the reward of being the best tipped the scale. I looked at the bout as another steppingstone to the optimum prize. Once the fight was written down in the books, I would be left to face only two more to reach the top.

The bell rang, and punches were thrown, and the kicks landed with purchase. As the seconds ticked off, I knew round one would be the only round in this fight. I felt it deep inside me.

I waited for an opening because I knew he

153

would allow one. My opponent kicked out, and I captured his leg and held it at my hip. I briefly thought of twisting it and dumping him to the mat. Instead, I held the leg and used the arm length advantage I had over my opponent and landed right punch after right punch. I made contact with his face, chest, stomach. I even switched the combination up, leaving him to gauge where he needed to block.

Blood poured from his mouth and ran down his neck to his chest. The cut above his eye was a hindrance no fighter needed. With his leg still held, I drove him back into the ropes. He bounced back toward me, and I released his leg and spun. My position changed and I stood behind him. I saw the referee eyeing my opponent to see if he was fit to go on.

The ref wasn't going to call it, the round too close to the end. I stepped up, locked my arm in a 'V' around his neck and held on as the fighter clawed my forearm. I increased the pressure until the clawing stopped, and the fighter's hands dropped to his side. The bout was mine.

The booing from the crowd hadn't even bothered me. I understood they wanted a longer fight. But as a fighter, I needed to take the shot that was given to me. I wouldn't chance whether I'd get another opening or not.

I looked to the corner and Teagan's smile was wide. O'Hagan's Gym swept their bouts.

After the win was officially given to me in a KO

154

and the hoopla was over, I grabbed my woman's hand and headed to the locker room.

We entered the room, and I locked my arms around her, spun, and pushed her against the door, slamming it in the process. I needed to feel her wrapped around me.

Finesse was nonexistent as I pulled her pants and panties down to the knees and then to the floor. She kicked her shoes off and stepped out of her clothing, and I backed her against the door, wrapped a hand around her thigh and lifted it to my hip, opening her to me. I pushed the front of my shorts down, jock and all with my free hand and my cock sprang free. I ran the tip through her folds to check to see if she was wet and when it slid with ease, I knew she would be able to take everything I wanted to give her.

I pushed in, and her head bent back against the door. Holding onto her thigh, I pounded in and out, the sound of her ass slapping the door. The harder I thrusted in, the louder she moaned.

Deeper. I needed to be deeper. I pulled out, her cry of frustration piercing my ears as I lifted her around her waist and moved us to the table, sitting her down. I slid her to the edge and onto my cock. The table banged against the wall with each of my thrusts as I buried myself to the hilt.

"I need... I..." was all she got out. I rested my hand against her mound and used my thumb to put pressure on her clit and rubbed. The move sent her over the edge with a scream, and the tightening of her core had my release shooting into her.

As we worked on our breaths, I leaned my head on her chest. "Did I hurt you, sweetheart?" I knew I was rough, but I had needed her badly.

"No, I enjoyed it," she said, causing my dick to twitch.

"Good, don't want you sore when we get back to the hotel," I said, pulling out and stepping back.

"It's nothing a nice warm bath won't fix. Let's gather up the stuff and then we can go find Nico and Shawn.

We left TD Garden behind us and headed to the hotel. New York and Las Vegas were the next two places where our journey would lead us. There would be plenty of time to focus on them once we were back in Chicago. Right then, I only wanted to concentrate on the woman beside me.

# Chapter Fifteen

## Teagan

The three wins in New York led to Vegas where three more wins set the guys up for the biggest fights of their lives. Every hour spent in the gym had been to reach the top. Shawn's, Nico's, and Max's blood, sweat, and tears had gotten them to that moment.

The ride to Hammond Civic Center had been quiet. Nico, Max, and Shawn sat in the back of the SUV while my dad and I sat up front, each one of the guys in their own heads. Today would be a history maker as O'Hagan's Gym had fighters in three of the eight World Championship fights. The biggest record of attendance had been tallied by the box offices. It had a part to do with the heavyweight fight between to homegrown boys: Maximum Masetti, the up and comer, versus Christoph Kiev, current belt holder.

"Are you doing okay, honey?" My dad patted my leg and smiled when I looked at him.

"Yes, but I don't know if it has truly sunk in. Do you know what is going to happen if they each take the belt in their class?" I whispered, not wanting anything to distract the men in the back.

"Teagan, it is going to happen no matter the results. You've taken three men, unknowns to boot, and in six months brought them to a level no one has ever reached so quickly." Dad drove while I let his words sink in.

"I had quality to work with," I said and turned back to stare out the passenger's side window.

"Ah, sweetheart, we were the ones to get quality." I turned around in my seat and smiled at Max's sweet words. He never failed to surprise me when he said stuff like that.

"Teagan, I wouldn't be here today if it wasn't for your determination. Kiev's told me I wouldn't make it past amateur status. If you hadn't seen me in a tournament, I never would have gotten so far," Shawn added, and leaned up from the third row to rest his arms on the back of the second-row seat.

"Shoot that first day we walked into O'Hagan's, I thought for sure we were going to get our asses handed to us before we got out of there because of Max," Nico said and hit Max with the back of his hand in the chest.

My dad chuckled. "That day I thought for sure Teagan's temper was going to reach a new level."

"As Max so eloquently put it that day, I am a

158

girl," I reminded everyone, and then the car filled with laughter.

"Got to rub up against you, didn't I?" Max pointed out, and I laughed, and Nico pinched his nose and closed his eyes.

"You can sleep on the couch tonight, but I'll be damned if I'm kept from our woman because you can't keep your mouth shut," Nico informed Max, and Max slapped Nico on his chest as payback.

"Enough! How many times do I have to say my daughter?" my dad asked, never taking his eyes off the road.

Max shrugged at me, Nico cracked his eyes open, and Shawn outright laughed.

"Really, now you play that card. The man who said they would be good for the gym." I grinned when he glanced in my direction and glowered. I put my hand up to stop the response I knew was coming. "I know, you are the parent."

"Damn straight, lassie, and don't forget it!" my dad boasted.

When we parked in the lot at the civic center, we were still laughing. It definitely eased the tension of what the evening was sure to hold for everyone involved.

We heard the crowd all the way into the locker rooms' area. The guys decided to share a room. I knew it was so I wouldn't have to move between the three. Shawn was up first, so his hands were taped, and he sat on the table in the zone.

159

Shawn hopped off the table when they announced the welterweight match.

"You got this, man," Nico said and patted Shawn's back.

"Only thing between you and the belt is twenty-five minutes," Max said, and he too patted Shawn's back. Then Nico and Max walked over to me.

"Best trainer around," Max whispered, leaned in, and captured my mouth with his. He broke the kiss and stepped back.

"Even though I'm a girl?" I questioned and smiled as my dad laughed. It wouldn't matter how long the three of us were together, I was never going to let Max forget his words from that first meeting.

"We like that you're a girl. It makes this not so awkward," Nico said, then chuckled against my lips as he too kissed me. The knock on the door signaled it was time and Nico stepped back.

Nico and Max each shook my dad's hand, then my dad, Shawn and I headed out the door. Max and Nico would stay in the room until it was time for their own fights.

The hallway was long, and with each step we took to the door that led into the main area, the sound of the crowd grew louder and louder. Security personnel opened the doors as we reached them.

I'd sat in the seats at title fights before, knew the crowd was loud, yet still, I never imagined to be

160

on this side of it all. My dad walked in front of Shawn, and I brought up the rear as we made our way down the aisle to the ring. I looked around at the crowd and spotted Max's and Nico's families. Everyone was in attendance, even Shawn's mom had come, and she was sitting beside Max's mom, Genieve.

"Twenty-five minutes, right?" Shawn said as he stepped into the ring.

"Or less. Up to you, son. Why don't you show them O'Hagan's puts out winners," Kearney O'Hagan said and smacked Shawn's shoulder. My dad had a way of saying just the right thing as I watched Shawn stand a little taller with the look of determination in his eyes.

"Remember, change it up. Crovto always leads with the left in everything: punches, kicks, you name it. Watch his hips, it will give you the direction he is going," Shawn nodded to everything I said. We continued to talk as the current belt holder, Danka Crovto, entered the ring. The referee called the fighters to the center and went through the standard repertoire as to what would be accepted and what wouldn't.

My dad moved beside me as the referee dropped his arm. Crovto bounced on the balls of his feet, and Shawn moved from side to side, each sizing up the other. I saw Crovto hips shift and knew he was going to move to his right. Shawn saw it, too. He adjusted and when Crovto made the first move, Shawn blocked the punch, knocking Crovto's

161

arm down. The next punch landed and caught Shawn in the ribs, the slight shift from Shawn told me it stung but nothing too painful.

The hit didn't keep Shawn from kicking out and landing a blow to Crovto's right knee. He stumbled, and Shawn was on him before he fully gained his balance back. Shawn landed consecutive punches before Crovto was able to put distance between himself and Shawn to gain back a little of his composure.

Round one ended. Which fighter took the round was up for grabs in my book.

Shawn stepped to his corner, and I handed him the bottled water. Dad wiped his face down. Nothing needed to be said, Shawn had executed his moves with precision.

Round two started. The round went much better for Crovto as he landed several blows and even took Shawn to the mat. Shawn bucked him off, landed a couple blows of his own, but the round was owned by Crovto.

Shawn moved to the corner. "Fucked that round up. I gave the bastard the advantage," Shawn said between drinks.

"It's only one round. Five minutes in time," I said and handed him a towel.

"Don't want to let you down, Teagan," Shawn announced as he wiped his face off.

"Knock that shit off. You could never let me down. You made it here, Shawn. I might have helped you fine tune some skills, but it's up to you to execute them. You won the fights that got you here. Now get in there and kick Crovto's ass and win this one. The belt needs a new owner," I encouraged, then grabbed the towel and water bottle from Shawn when he stood.

Shawn fought more aggressively in the third round. He performed a roundhouse kick, and if Crovto hadn't moved quickly on his feet, the graze would have been the knockout blow Shawn had been setting up. The round ended and it had to go to Shawn, no other way it could have gone. Water was handed over, his face and arms were wiped down, and then he was back in the center.

Crovto must have gotten chewed out in his corner because he went for Shawn immediately as round four kicked off. He led with his left leg and kicked out, it landed on Shawn's right side. The next kick was with his right, and he made contact with Shawn's left side. Shawn blocked the left-right combination punches that followed and came back at Crovto with his own combo. Right, right, left. Left, left, right. Each punch Shawn landed moved Crovto back a step.

My dad placed his hand on my shoulder and squeezed. I realized then that I had been literally bouncing on my feet. The crowd got to their feet. It was if they sensed the end was near, but no one knew who was going to prevail.

Shawn caught a blow to the cheek that sent his head to the side. He shook it off and delivered his own. Kicks were exchanged, punches, each fighter looked for an opening. Crovto stepped to the side, his leg came out and up, his foot aimed for Shawn's chin. The hand on my shoulder tightened, and I knew my dad saw what I did. The fight was going to end right there. The crowd had been right and as they grew louder, I figured they knew it, too.

Crovto's foot was inches from its mark, Shawn saw it coming, and as if time stopped, Shawn had Crovto's ankle in his hand, and his leg extended out. He brought Crovto's leg to his hip and held on for leverage as he kicked with his other leg. Shawn's foot made contact with Crovto's chin; their positions had reversed. Shawn went for the KO kick and landed it perfectly. Blood splattered out of Crovto's mouth as his head snapped back from the blow.

Shawn let go of Crovto's leg and since it was the only thing keeping Crovto upright. When the leg dropped, so did Crovto. His body bounced once, and then he laid motionless on the mat. The referee moved in and the crowd erupted. There was a new welterweight champion. My whole body vibrated as I watched Shawn's arm raised to signal the win. He was handed the belt, and I moved toward him. When he faced me, the grin on his face would have lit the entire city it was so bright. He grabbed me up in his arms and swung me around as he had done every time he won. It had turned into a ritual of sorts. When he put me down, my dad shook his hand and then pulled Shawn into a hug.

Kearney O'Hagan had to be feeling what I felt—a new beginning for O'Hagan's. On our way back to the locker rooms, they announced the middleweight fight and the fighters. One was from Kiev's Gym, and he too was trying to unseat the champion who held the belt.

When we reached the door to the room, Shawn busted in, held the belt over his head, and Nico and Max shared in his accomplishment.

"Hot damn, one down," Max yelled, and lifted Shawn off his feet, then dropped him.

"Knew you could do it," Nico said and repeated Max's move with Shawn.

"There was a minute there I thought he had me," Shawn said and shook his head. "I want to be ringside for both of your fights. I'm going to hit the shower and put on regular street clothes. Wouldn't want all the single ladies to recognize me and start a riot." He laughed as he walked toward the bathroom in the back of the room.

"We heard the crowd go crazy, but we couldn't quite make out any of the words being yelled," Max said and sat back down on the table.

"Shawn did great," my dad said and continued to talk to Max and Nico about the fight. I sat down and listened as he went over each move the fighters had done. I leaned my head back against the wall and closed my eyes to let it all sink in. Shawn won the championship belt, but the gym would get advertising for producing the fighter.

The announcement was made for the light

165

heavyweight bout. Nico looked at me and smiled. I loved him so much. Both of them. As if Max sensed something was wrong, he turned away from my dad and looked at me.

"What's wrong?" Max asked.

I shook my head. "Nothing. It's almost time for Nico's fight to start," I replied, and Max stood and walked over to me.

"Are you worried about us winning?" Nico asked as he joined Max in front of me.

"Not at all."

"Good. I think I can speak for both of us. Today we might walk away as champions, but it doesn't change the fact that the day we met you, we'd already won." Tears filled my eyes at Max's words, and I stood and jumped into his arms.

"I love you both so much," I said against his neck, and he squeezed me tight.

"I love you, too, sweetheart." Max kissed the side of my head and then handed me off to Nico.

"Teagan, you're more than either of us could have hoped for. I love you, baby," Nico said and laid a soft kiss on my lips. The knock on the door had him pulling back before he could deepen it. "Damn, what is up with the knocking when I'm trying to kiss our girl?" He looked down at me and smiled. "Let's go win another belt, baby."

When the door opened the three of us turned to see my dad and Shawn standing in the doorway.

"It's time. I thought I better interrupt in case you hadn't heard the knock," my dad said and

166

grinned at us.

"What are you doing in the hall?" I asked and furrowed my brows. I hadn't even noticed he left or that Shawn had come out of the shower.

"We wanted to give you three some privacy. Now we need to get out there," my dad answered and pointed over his shoulder with his thumb.

"Yeah, we're coming." When I turned back, Max was hugging Nico, and he whispered something that I couldn't make out. Then Nico turned to walk toward the door.

"What was that?" I asked Max.

"I told him whoever won their fight in the least amount of time, would be the one to marry you legally." My mouth dropped open at Max's answer. When I looked over my shoulder, Nico had a big smile on his face, and my dad and Shawn were trying not to laugh. I turned back to face Max.

"Really? You're going to wager who gets to marry me." I glared at Max, the man was infuriating at times.

"Teagan, we need to go. You can argue with Max later," my dad said, and I turned to see him grinning as he looked at Max, then at Nico who was chuckling beside him. I was outnumbered, but they were right, it wasn't the time.

"We already cleared it with your dad, Teagan. He likes the idea," Max advised with a huge grin, and I looked at my dad who shrugged. His grin mirrored Max's.

"You are all assholes," I said and stomped

167

toward the door and passed Nico and my dad without stopping to see if they followed.

"Yet, you love us!" Max yelled as the door closed to the locker room, and we continued to walk down the hall.

I shook my head. Yes, I did love them. There would never be an argument on that.

# Chapter Sixteen

## Nico

As I stood and waited for the referee to drop his arm for the fight to begin, I looked over to my corner and to the woman who had come to mean so much to me in a short time. I might have had the dream to be there one day, but she was the one who made it all worthwhile. With her love and support, there was nothing Max nor I couldn't do.

I focused back on the referee and shut out the crowd and everything around me except my opponent. The only thing between me and the light heavyweight belt was Evan Michaels and five rounds, five minutes each. The arm of the referee dropped, and my single goal of winning started. I charged Evan and came in low, wrapped my arms around his thighs, and dumped him to the mat, landing on top of him. Evan rolled from side to side and bucked his hips knocking me off. We both scrambled to our feet and circled one another.

Evan landed two blows, one to my side and the other on my cheek. I saw that one coming and adjusted for it, minimizing the blow but I wasn't quite fast enough as Evan's knuckles grazed my cheek. I countered with my own set of punches followed by a kick to Evan's ribs.

Round one was over as quick as it started.

"You're doing great, Nico. He's feeling the kick to the ribs," Teagan talked while I drank water and wiped my face down with the rag Kearney handed me.

"He would have cut my cheek wide open if that one blow had landed full force," I mentioned, then took another big drink, and the water felt good sliding down my throat.

"It's only a scratch," Teagan said as round two was announced.

I stood and moved to the center. The round started with a kick from Evan that was going to leave a nice sized bruise on my thigh, it stung like the devil, but I kept my balance and returned the favor. My blow landed on his hip and threw him off balance. As he battled to gain it back, I took advantage and shifted sideways, kicking out. The blow to the chest sent him into the ropes and then down to the mat just as round two ended.

"Nico, you're better than him. That round was yours, and so was the first round. Now stop dancing with him and get the job done," Teagan said and handed me the bottle of water. I took a gulping drink and looked up at her.

"Do you want to marry me, baby? All you had to do was say so," I teased, stood, and handed the water bottle to her. Kearney chuckled and had to pull Teagan away from the ropes, her mouth hung open. It had to be the first time she'd been struck speechless.

Round three started and it had both Evan and I taking turns on the mat. His kick and my single leg sweep took him down to the mat, and I followed to get a few good blows in before he bucked me off. Evan caught me setting up my next move and before I could complete the roundhouse, he grabbed me from behind, and we landed on the mat together. He only got one blow in before I rose, knocking him to the side.

The rest of the round was even with punches and kicks, some that landed, and some that only touched air. Our bodies would be sore tomorrow, but right then, the adrenaline pumped through our blood. At the end of the round, I felt it could go either way. We each had spent time blocking the other's combination shots.

"Your footwork is some of the best I've seen, Nico. Use it," Teagan said and stepped away, and I looked toward Kearney.

"The belt is all but yours, son. You only need to reach for it," Kearney said and moved to where Teagan stood. I took the last seconds before the next round and looked toward the crowd and found my father staring at me as the rest of our family members sat around him. His grin told me everything. Win or lose, the family support and love would always be there. I turned back, stood, and walked to the center of the ring—as Kearney said, the bout was mine to win or lose. The only one to control the end result was me.

Round four started, and Evan came at me with consecutive punches that I blocked. The next was a kick, which landed on my thigh. I staggered, but the blow wasn't hard enough to take me down. After I had gained my balance, it was my turn to go for him. I advanced but he was ready for the kick out from my side, and he countered. His kick landed at the back of my knee and it buckled, taking me to the mat. Evan came in for the pin, straddled my back and went for my arms to keep me from pushing up off the mat. With my arms pinned at my back and his weight pushed down on me, the count was all that was left, and I would be done.

I rocked my hips, but with the way his legs were positioned on the outside of me, I got no purchase from the rocking.

"Throw him off, Nico. You're better, damn it!" I heard Teagan yell. My name was shouted from the crowd and from the direction the voices were coming from, I'm sure it was my family.

"This is what happens when you have a female training you." It was the first time doing the bout that Evan had spoken and right as the referee began the countdown. Evan would think later he should have stayed silent until it was over.

The move was going to temporarily hurt like a motherfucker but if I succeeded, it would be so worth the strain on my body. I arched my back, my chest raised from the mat and with my arms held behind, my shoulders wanted to resist the move. The referee had hit five in the countdown to my defeat, but the move made Evan adjust to shift more of his weight forward to keep my torso down. When he did, the weight on my hips lightened and enabled me, with the use of my legs, to raise me enough on one side to have him start to slip from my body.

Evan tried to hang on, but there was no use. The referee said nine, and with the last of my momentum, I tossed him from my body. The release on my arms, though they felt weak from being in the odd position, allowed me to push to my knees, which gave me the extra I needed to get upright on my feet before ten was said.

The look on Evan's face was priceless as his eyes tracked my movements while he rose to his feet. I gave him no time to react. I delivered punch after punch, and he couldn't keep the majority from landing. Blood oozed from his nose and lip. The round couldn't have much time left to it, and I wanted it over. When I saw his body sway, I backed away, performed a one-eighty with my leg out, then I turned back, and my foot made contact under his arm, the power behind the kick more than enough to drop him. With him off balance, I moved in and grabbed him around the neck. The

173

'V' hold put pressure on his neck, and he wouldn't last long before the blood flow to his brain ceased, and he would be out cold.

"No, this is what having a woman train you is like," I said as Evan grabbed at my arms, shifted his body, and tried to use anything to get me to loosen my hold. When he tapped out, nothing could have been sweeter.

Even after the bout was called, the win mine by submission, hadn't felt complete until I had Teagan in my arms. She hugged me tightly with no worry for the sweat or blood that graced my body. My family was on their feet clapping and cheering. My dad's face still held a grin only bigger and anyone who saw it would have been able to read it. It was the one that said 'that is my boy.'

"I knew you could do it, son," Kearney said and patted me on the back.

"I'm so proud of you, Nico," Teagan said when I set her back on her feet.

"Couldn't have done it without you, baby," I answered and kissed her on the forehead.

After I received the belt and pics were taken, Shawn, Teagan, Kearney, and I walked back to the locker room. They'd already announced about the heavyweight bout being next. When we opened the door and entered, Max rose from the chair.

"Well? Don't keep me hanging. I heard a lot of yelling out there," Max said, and I was shocked he had been sitting down instead of pacing. It was a usual thing for him.

174

"Really, you need to ask?" I questioned and held up the belt. He charged across the room and grabbed me up in a hug.

"Damn, two down, one more to go. We're going to sweep this fucker," Max said enthusiastically.

"No losses," everyone said in unison.

"Ready for yours?" Teagan asked.

"You bet I am. The wait for my bout is what has been hardest," Max said just as the knock sounded, indicating it was time.

"Are you coming out after you shower?" Max asked.

"I'll shower after yours. Just going to throw on my clothes and I will be out there. Don't want to miss you taking down Christoph," I answered.

"Me, too. There are extra chairs on the floor by the contenders' corners. I sat there for Nico's bout," Shawn said.

"We got to go, Max," Teagan said and walked over to kiss me before she headed toward the door with Max and her dad behind her.

When Max reached the door, he paused and turned around. "What was your time?"

"Eighteen minutes twenty-three seconds," I smirked.

"Oh for God's sake, come on," Teagan groused, shook her head, and pulled on Max's arm.

"What? It just means I have to be done by eighteen twenty-two, and I am one golden heavyweight champion with a future wife," Max said.

Teagan's sigh and Kearney's and Shawn's laughter was the last thing I heard as the door closed.

# Chapter Seventeen

## Max

The walk to the ring was loud as some cheered and some booed. When my name was yelled, I turned and saw my family. They've been behind Nico and me from the beginning, pushing us, supporting us, picking up the slack at work so we could train. Family was everything when it came to the Masetti's and Asaro's groups. I looked over at Teagan, she was the unexpected surprise in all of this. Without her, I wasn't sure we would have gotten the opportunity. But if I had to choose between any of it, I would gladly give it up just to have her. A career in the MMA was short. Belts and titles changed from one bout to the next. However, Teagan was our future. When she caught me looking at her, she smiled, and that simple gesture from her gave me the needed calm. I winked and turned back to face the center of the ring more at

177

peace than I had been only a second before. It was my time, I felt it deep in my bones. Whether in twenty-five minutes or five, at the end the belt would belong to me.

I bounced on my toes and waited for Christoph to arrive in the ring. Kiev was the current owner of the belt for the heavyweight class. Christoph was good, I was better. I had strength, I had the skill, and I had Teagan O'Hagan for a trainer. After tonight, no one would ever say, 'but she's a girl,' including me.

Cheers rang out, and I turned my head to watch Christoph as he made his way to the ring. From the outside, he seemed cool and collected, the inside was what I was going to take advantage of. I continued to bounce on my toes as they announced our stats. I had a longer reach than him, which would pay off in distance for me, but not up close. Up close shots would be his one and only advantage. When the announcers stopped talking, we moved to the center with the referee. I ran my eyes over Christoph, the ten pounds and two inches I had on him was evident while close to each other.

The referee stepped back, and round one started.

Christoph came at me and wrapped me up, trying for an immediate takedown to the mat. The strength in my body outweighed his determination.

"Not bad, Masetti, just won't be enough," Christoph boasted as he tried to move me

178

backward.

"It's enough to take the belt from you," I grounded out and used my leg strength to move him back. When I had him at the ropes, I alternated between legs, bringing them up to each of his sides, battering his midsection with the contact. He released me, and before he could get his body in an upright position, I swung my leg up, the blow to his face from my knee had blood spraying.

Christoph came up swinging and snapped my head back with an uppercut. I tasted blood in my mouth, and it would have been a lot worse if we weren't required to wear mouthpieces. He switched to punches, rotating between face and stomach, which placed me on defense as I blocked. All that was needed was to keep them from landing until he changed up. No way would he be able to keep at his current pace. I'd give him this round, but it cost him energy.

One round done.

"What were you doing?" Teagan asked as I sat on the chair and drank from the water bottle that had been handed to me. After I had finished, I used the towel Kearney dropped in my lap to wipe my face and Christoph's blood off my leg.

"I was blocking. He won't be able to keep that pace each round."

"He shouldn't even be given a chance to set that type of pace. Stick to your own attack plan. Make him go on the defensive," Teagan scolded, and I nodded.

The minutes between rounds ticked off quick and round two started with me going for the bodylock. I wrapped him up and took us both to the mat. We rolled several times, neither of us able to get the advantage. Stuck with only the blows to our bodies. I was able to push him away, which gave me space and time to get back to my feet. As Christoph rose, I kicked out. The blow to his chest sent him back into the ropes where I met him full force with my fists. The time spent on the speed bag had definitely paid off. The succession of punches was difficult for Christoph to block. When the bell was rung, he was bleeding from the nose again, his mouth, and a cut above his eye.

"That round belongs to you. You've got him, Max. Fifteen minutes left. Three rounds. If you stay at him, the bout is yours," Teagan said as I drank water and toweled off.

"Eight twenty-two," I said, handed the water bottle and towel to Kearney and stood. Nico's laugh had me looking to the chairs off to the side where he and Shawn sat.

"What?" Teagan asked as she looked at Nico, then back to me.

"You're marrying me, sweetheart. Nico knows it," I said and walked to the center of the ring, leaving Teagan with her mouth open and being pulled away by Kearney.

Three started, and Christoph came at me. He went low, wrapped my legs and took me down, then he scrambled to straddle me. I arched my back, lifting my hips off the mat and rotated. He fell to the side and shifted until I straddled him. He punched at my sides and bucked. The forearm I threw had Christoph turned his head. I dropped the forearm to his neck and applied pressure. The move would have had others tapping out, but Christoph was anything but weak. He bucked and punched until he tossed me off. When I hit the mat, I moved out of his reach and stood. Christoph bounced to his feet, and the bell rang as we both threw punches that never came close to landing.

"That round was pretty even. You're down to ten minutes. You need to make every contact to his body count in these next two rounds," Teagan advised.

"Three twenty-two," I smirked.

"Stop it! I am not discussing that in the ring anymore. Stop worrying about the bet with Nico and get the damn job done," Teagan said and walked away. I looked up at Kearney, and he grinned and shook his head and took the towel and water bottle I handed him.

"After you marry her, son—you might not want to close your eyes when you sleep," Kearney said and stepped back. I moved forward for the fourth round with his laughter ringing in my ears.

For a brief second, I wondered if any other fighters had this much fun at the fights, then Christoph kicked out, and my focus went right on him. I grabbed his leg but didn't get him dumped before he twisted out of my grasp. We exchanged kicks, punches, and each had a takedown to the mat. The round was even in my mind but, that didn't mean the three judges would agree.

Seconds were ticking off into minutes, and I needed to make my move. I went for Christoph, swinging, and kept the distance, using my arm reach advantage, which kept Christoph at bay. I needed him to react like I knew he would—and he did. The lunge forward brought him closer, and he even landed a few punches to my mid-section. With his shoulders slightly hunched forward and his head lowered, I brought my fist up, clipped his chin with enough power to snap his head back. While he staggered backward, I twisted my hips, kicked out and up, and the bottom of my foot made contact with his chin.

When Christoph's head snapped back that time, it was enough. He fell to the mat, and his head bounced once. The KO was mine along with the belt. I'd done it, World Heavyweight Champion. Well, at least until I was challenged again. However, I planned to keep it as long as possible.

The referee raised my arm, I was handed the belt, and the announcer ran through the scoring until leading up to the KO. The grin that split my face actually hurt it was so big. The KO happened fourth round and eighteen minutes nineteen seconds into the bout.

I looked over at Teagan who had one of the commission's men talking with her. She looked over at me and shook her head. Nico's 'lucky bastard' came from behind me, followed by Kearney's chuckle and a slap on my back.

Our families stood on the floor around the ring and waited. When the announcements and presentation were over, they too flooded the ring to congratulate not only me but Nico and Shawn, too.

"I'm proud of you, son," my dad said as he hugged me while Uncle Vinnie did the same to Nico.

After, our brothers and sisters got just enough time to congratulate us before my mom and Aunt Angelina shoved them out of the way to do their inspections.

"I'm alright, Mom," I said when she reached up and grabbed my face and turned it side to side.

"Maximum, hold still. I need to see for myself. You may be a grown man, but you will always be my baby. It was hard enough sitting nicely and watching your baby get hit." I looked over at my dad for help, and he shrugged.

"Roll with it, son. Be thankful I held her in her seat, or your opponent might have been KO'd in the first round. At the very least he would have been maimed."

Teagan finished talking with the man from the commission and walked over with a huge smile on her face as she watched my mother.

"Enough, Mom. You can inspect every bruise and bump later. Trust me, in a couple hours I'm sure more spots will be visible," I told her, and when she let go of my face, I grabbed Teagan and pulled her into my side.

"We are going to maneuver everyone out of here, bro," my oldest brother, Joe, said loud enough for the parents to hear. Then he leaned in, "They're planning a celebration. I'll get them to put it off until tomorrow, but you are going to owe me. I might need you to do the same for me one day," he whispered.

"You got it, Joe. Anytime. Love ya, bro," I said, and Teagan laughed and kissed Joe's cheek, and I heard her whispered 'thank you.'

"You and Nico take my sister-in-law-to-be home," Joe said and grinned.

"Really, how the hell do you know already?" I asked, and Joe laughed and shook his head. "What?"

"Don't make me question that you might be adopted. You've been around this family for fuck's sake. Nothing gets by them," Joe smirked. I nodded in agreement because he was right. No one kept shit to themselves in our family and even if they tried, someone always found out.

I felt Teagan's body start to shake and I looked down at her, and her head was bowed as she tried hiding her laughter.

"Plus, you and Nico forgot that everything echoes when you are in an empty building," Joe informed.

"Fucker," I mumbled and shook my head. Joe laughed, then turned and started the roundup of our family.

"You going to give me a kiss, sweetheart?" I asked, and when Teagan looked up at me, I bent my head to close the distance between us. I captured her lips, and as always, it was like coming home.

# Chapter Eighteen

## Nico

Everyone wanted to celebrate, including us, but just in another way. A party of three and a celebration it would be. There would be plenty of time to celebrate with family later. Max might get to marry Teagan on paper, but my commitment to her would be nonetheless real. Max and I already had the contract done, which would give her security in our relationship no matter what took place. It even went into detail about any children we'd have between the three of us. Family was family, and it wouldn't matter which one of us, Max or me, fathered the child. Bottom line, she was ours and any children we were lucky enough to have, would be, too. Any other details would be minor ones.

Teagan pulled the car in the garage, no one had even spoken after we dropped Shawn and

Kearney off. The adrenaline and the fact that within six short months, not only had we reached a goal—we won the relationship jackpot, and she currently entered the house.

I looked at Max, and he nodded as we both watched Teagan's ass as she walked in front of us. We no sooner entered the kitchen when Max tossed his bag on the table, the thud the only sound heard.

"You're going to damage the table doing that," Teagan said when she turned around at the sound. She reached for the bag, I assumed to move it, but she didn't get the chance. Max bent at the waist and put his shoulder into Teagan's stomach and lifted her off her feet. "What are you doing?"

"Ah, sweetheart, do you have to ask," Max said and slapped her ass. She squealed and pinched Max's butt and raised her head to look up at me as I followed Max through the house and up the stairs.

"Let me explain it to you, baby. For the last week, you have been telling us *'After the fights, you need every ounce of strength.'* We gave you that because of the 'her way or no way' deal. The fights are done, and our strength and stamina are being fueled by adrenaline so...it's now going to be 'our way and every way.'" Her eyes went wide and were glued to me.

"Fuck me, she likes that idea, Nico. She just shuddered and..." Max paused inside the door of the bedroom and turned to face me, one of his hands that held her, rubbed over her ass and between her thighs. He moved it back and forth, and she squirmed, causing him to tighten his hold to keep from dropping her. "Oh yeah, the heat coming from her pussy tells me she likes that idea a lot. Bet when we strip her those little panties she likes to wear off, they are damp." Teagan wiggled her hips and tried to close her legs with Max's hand caught between her thighs.

"I'm not wearing panties," came out on a pant from Teagan and I was sure Max was going to drop her as he moved quickly to the bed.

"Christ, hurry up and get her naked before I blow in my pants. If my dick gets any harder, it's going to bust the zipper on my jeans," as I spoke my shirt was over my head and tossed on the floor with my pants not far behind. Max set Teagan on the bed and stepped back to remove his clothes. I wasn't about to wait, "I got her," was all I said as I reached for her.

Teagan's shirt was first and then her jeans as I yanked them down her legs. She laid there watching wearing only her bra. I unclasped it, pulled the straps down her arms, and tossed it to join the rest of the clothes that littered the bedroom carpet.

"You couldn't be more perfect, baby," I said as I ran my fingers down her cheek to her neck, down between her breasts, then circled them before I continued down to her belly button. Goosebumps trailed my fingers, and her body twitched as I

189

continued to move down. When I reached her mound and slipped my fingers between her folds, I found her wet. The moan she released when I pushed my fingers in and applied pressure to her clit with the heel of my hand, had my cock throbbing.

"Watching you come apart as Nico finger fucks you has my dick ready to burst, sweetheart," Max said and moved to the side and leaned over her chest and took one of her nipples in his mouth. It must have been what she needed because Teagan threw her head back and screamed my name as the evidence of her orgasm flooded my hand. We didn't allow her time to recover. I pulled my fingers out of her pulsing pussy and dropped to my knees, pushed her legs wide so I could settle between them and lowered my mouth to her. The taste of her on my tongue had me craving more as I licked and nipped at her.

Small tremors still racked her body as Max moved up on the bed and knelt back on his knees above her head. As I continued my assault on her, he supported her head as he tilted it back and fed her his cock.

Teagan wasted no time as her mouth opened wide and Max's dick slowly disappeared inside. Needing more of her, I used my fingers, spread her lips, and pushed my tongue in. As I mimicked Max's motion with my tongue, I took one hand and moved to her clit and pinched the hard nub between two fingers. The reward was another orgasm, and the cream coated my tongue. After I had licked her clean, I stood, raised her legs until her feet rested against my pecs, and my cock hovered at her entrance. In one thrust I was buried deep within her. Pausing to give her time to adjust to the invasion, I rested a hand on her mound and used my thumb to rub her clit.

Max showed her no mercy as I watched him pump in and out of her mouth, but our woman didn't seem to mind, not when I saw her bend her neck back as far as she could, and her throat muscles worked to swallow. The sight of her with Max's cock in her mouth so far that his balls touched her face, had my hips moving. I pulled back until the head of my cock was the only thing inside her, then slammed back into the hilt. We worked Teagan from both ends, and she took everything we gave her.

"Sonofabitch!" Max yelled before his body jerked and I knew he lost the battle with her mouth, same as I lost it inside her core. I felt my balls draw up and I pulled out and thrusted in one last time. Her body trembled with yet another orgasm, coating my cock as I emptied into her.

Teagan released Max's dick with a pop, and I pulled out of her. She moaned and laid motionless other than her chest rising and falling as she tried to catch her breath.

She moaned when I leaned over her, kissed her stomach, and placed my hands on her breasts and squeezed. Teagan's nipples hardened to peaks as I ran my hands back and forth over them.

"Going to have to get these pierced with some hoops, baby, so we can watch them bounce when we fuck you." Teagan's legs shifted under me, her thighs rubbing together. "You like that, huh?" When she didn't answer me, Max leaned his face over hers.

"We're not done, sweetheart," he said and leaned down and kissed her. Her response to him was instant. I watched them kissing and continued to play with her breasts. The longer it went on, the more she shifted her hips around. My dick throbbed as it stood at attention again and I stopped the play and moved my hands from her breasts. I moved to the side and then got on the bed and positioned myself on my back.

"Slide her up here, Max. I don't know about you, but I am ready to go again." Teagan moaned when Max released her mouth. He moved his hands under her arms and slid her up beside me. I patted her leg. "Come on, baby, need you wrapped around me."

"How can you two be ready again?" she asked but moved to straddle me and when her pussy slid over my cock, we both groaned.

"Adrenaline is a beautiful thing," I commented and lifted her then brought her back down and impaled her in one move. Teagan rocked her hips, and I reached up and tweaked her nipples. The sounds she emanated had Max reaching for the lube.

Max moved in position behind Teagan after he lubed his cock. "Hold her still while I get her ready to take me," he said, and I pulled her down until she rested on my chest and held her by the hips as Max prepared her. I knew she was ready when she tried to push back toward him. Her breasts rubbed down my chest and she groaned.

"Greedy girl wants my cock," Max said and worked his way in, pushing her further down on me.

I took her mouth, and Max started to move behind her. As Max pushed in, I pulled back. Teagan broke our kiss to pant as we took her slow. Before long we set a pace that had each of us breathing hard.

"I'm fucking close, man. She is tight as hell around my cock," Max gritted out.

"I'm with you, man. Come on, baby, take what you need and pull us over the edge with you," I encouraged, and she did. She slammed down on me as Max thrust in from behind and the three of us came together.

Max leaned his head on her back while hers rested on my chest. When our breathing leveled out, Max pulled out and collapsed to the side. Teagan moved off me and laid between us. After a minute or two passed, Max got out of bed and went to the bathroom, and when he came out, he brought a warm cloth and cleaned Teagan up.

He tossed the cloth back in the direction of the bathroom, then settled back into the bed. Teagan

193

rolled over and placed her head back on my chest.

I closed my eyes and enjoyed the feel of her. With the knowledge that no matter what happened in our lives from here on out, we'd end each day like this—I let sleep pull me under.

# Epilogue

## Teagan

*One year later...*

I held my finger to my lips as Max and Nico turned the corner and started walking up the hall. They joined me outside the partially closed door.

We stood there silently and listened as my dad was singing a song. One I remembered from my childhood that he used to sing to me. With his back to the door, he had no knowledge we were there as we listened and watched him rock his grandson.

When he finished singing, he reached to the table beside the rocker and picked up a tiny set of boxing gloves and held them up for Cory.

"I'll teach you everything you need to know about boxing. Your daddies and mama can teach you the other skills needed for the MMA. Between the four of us, there won't be anything you can't do." Cory gurgled as if he agreed, and my dad chuckled, then added.

"But one important thing to remember when it comes to your mama—it is Her Way or No Way."

# About the Author

Carson Mackenzie enjoys writing romance with a real feel to the stories. She writes with the belief not every man is a jerk and not every woman needs saving.

Carson lives in the South with her son, a Great Dane and two adopted shelter dogs that keep the household in line. Books have always been a part of her life. There is nothing better to her than curling up and relaxing with a good story and losing herself in someone else's world for a few hours.

Writing stories and growing as an author with each book is her goal. She wants to reach the level where a reader knows when they see her name on a cover, they can trust in the fact there will be a good story as they flip through the pages.

Carson's journey into writing has been for several years, and she's just finally starting to settle in. She can't believe she waited so long to start.

To stay up to date with Carson – you can follow on her <u>Website</u> or sign up for her <u>Newsletter</u>.

# Books by Carson Mackenzie

### Black Hawk MC

Speed
Crusher
Devil
Ghost
Jag
Coast
Flirt
Flyboy & Preacher - TBA

### Boxed Sets

Black Hawk MC Books 1-3

### Haven MC

Snatched

## Desert Phoenix MC

## Standalones